THE MAGICAL SUMMER GARDEN

KIRSTY FERRY

The Schubert Series Book 6

ChocLit

A JOFFE BOOKS COMPANY

Choc Lit
A Joffe Books company
www.choc-lit.com

First published in Great Britain in 2023

ISBN: 978-1-78189-530-6

To my family, with love.

ACKNOWLEDGMENTS

Welcome to the sixth book in the Schubert series! When I wrote book five, It Started with a Wedding, I thought that might have been the last one — but I underestimated Schubert and his legions of fans, who all made it pretty clear that he needed more stories. He wasn't meant to be in this one. But he is. And how could I deny him? This time he's sharing the animal limelight with a honey bee called Bertie, and I think they get on quite well . . .

Bea's Garden, which is based on Dilston Physic Garden in Corbridge, Northumberland, first appeared in It Started with a Wedding, and I knew as soon as I created the lilac-haired Bea that she and The Man from the Big House needed their own book; so here it is! I do hope you enjoy it, and Schubert would also like it to be known that he doesn't think this is the tail-end of his tales. Let's see if he's correct.

Huge thanks must go to my wonderful publisher Choc Lit, my fantastic editor and my amazing cover designer. The Tasting Panel (especially Katy Clarke, Kate Avetoomyan, Lydia Groenewald, Carol Botting, Janice Butler, Alan Roberton, Jenny Mitchell, Cheryl Woodbridge, Julie Lilly, Laura Sumner, Fran Stevens, Jo Osborne, Barbara Temple, Brigette Hughes, Emily Smeby, Lynda Adcock, Honor

Gilbert, Lorna Baker and Gill Leivers) and the Choc Lit Stars have, as ever, been invaluable in bringing this book to publication, and I also need to thank my family and friends for their love and support — as always.

CHAPTER ONE

Bea

So you may wonder why you've caught me like this — "this" being perched astride a high garden wall, which was probably best before 1800, dressed in a bumble bee outfit. I've even got the deely-boppers to match. And don't let Nature fool you — if bees are as fat as I am in this outfit, it should be totally impossible for them to fly. Fact.

I'm not flying though. I'm not going anywhere. My cousin, Fae, is standing looking up at me, alongside the hugest, fattest, blackest cat I've ever encountered. Fae is making helpful comments like, 'Shall we get you a zip wire? Would you like to come down that way, Cousin Bea? Because if you do, then Alfie will probably be able to work out the maths and triangulate it, and fashion a zip wire in no time, and then you can come down right in the middle of your beehives, and that will look, really, really cool.'

Alfie is Fae's boyfriend. He's good at science and triangulating and things, but his many scientific talents aren't really going to be helpful to me at this very moment in time.

'Mow wow,' says the cat, and then Fae says, 'Yes, Schubert, you could probably have a go on it as well. We could fashion you a little harness, and then you—'

1

'Shut up, Fae!' I mutter between gritted teeth. 'I've almost got him in sight.' "Him" being The Man who lives in the Big House on the other side of the wall. 'I'm not going anywhere yet.'

I think I can vaguely make out a figure walking around the perimeter of the house, but they are quite a distance away, because the house is quite a way up the lawn so I'm not certain exactly who I'm seeing.

It honestly seemed like a great idea to dress up and have some publicity photos taken for my garden — Bea's Garden; my very own garden, named after me — which is an area that used to be the walled garden of the Big House over there. Hence the dividing wall.

I bought the plot of land a few years ago, with the intention of turning the place into a very special garden. I knew that at some point in its past it had been part of the wider Glentavish Estate, but it had since been separated into two properties; one property was the house and the estate, and the other property was what is now my Garden. I'm sure the house and estate have many more exciting outbuildings than I have here, but I do have a very sweet Visitors' Hut to welcome people, and it's extremely cosy on cold days. The Hut also smells divine inside, as it's stocked up with herbal and floral products made with plants grown in the Garden.

One of the things that had attracted me to the Garden and the estate was the knowledge that a stunningly beautiful woman called Lady Clementine Eliza Grey used to live at Glentavish House. I'd come across her name in a booklet published by the Local History Society, and as my middle name is Clementine, I'd felt an instant connection. There aren't many of us around, in my experience. To delight me even further, apparently she was a keen garden designer, just like me. Plus, there was a rather winsome sketch of Lady Clementine in the booklet, allegedly done by her husband just after they were married, and I loved it. So, when the opportunity came up to buy the land, I didn't hesitate. To me, it was meant to be. The booklet said Lady Clementine

2

had died before her landscaping had been completed, and an extract from one of her letters had included talk of follies yet to be built, and the idea of a grand gateway linking the formal gardens with the walled garden.

I've worked hard on my little enterprise, originally intending to honour Lady Clementine's plans and recreate her dream — but as so often happens, I've discovered the Garden has its own agenda and I basically have to go with it. Now I grow healing plants in Bea's Garden, and nurture plants with magical properties here too. But I have yet to build any follies or discover the grand gateway.

The Garden is set out in a higgledy-piggledy fashion, guiding the visitors through lots of different areas, dotted with all sorts of interesting objects and notice boards. I've even got a small Poison Garden, and a Witches and Warlocks' Garden; a particular favourite of Fae's. Her boyfriend, Alfie, has two nieces, Isabel and Maggie May, who love that area too, and sometimes they bring Schubert, Alfie's sister's cat — the beast who is sitting at Fae's feet today. Schubert, Fae says, feels "particularly at home" here.

I've never asked Fae how she knows that.

And I don't ask Fae why Schubert is with her today — I'm used to her randomly turning up with him and saying she's cat-sitting; I just accept him now.

Currently, both Fae and Schubert are still staring up at me quizzically. Fae — and Schubert as well, for all I know — is also still making "helpful" suggestions.

'Perhaps you can try to fly down, Cousin Bea? I mean, I know it should be against the rules of bee-dom, but if bees can fly, maybe Bea can fly? Or at least drop gracefully into the honeysuckle.'

'Mow wow,' adds Schubert.

'I'm not dropping anywhere and I'm certainly not flying. And I'm really not stuck.'

'Well, we finished taking photos a little while ago,' offers Fae. 'And I think you dressed as a bee will certainly add to the allure of the garden and your honey, but I don't think I can go home and leave you sitting on that wall, so we'd best think of a way to get you down—'

'For the umpteenth time, I'm not stuck,' I reiterate. 'I'm spying.'

'Spying?'

'Mow wow?'

'Yes! I'm spying on The Man.'

I've never actually seen The Man. All I've had is a series of moany, whingy notes from him complaining that my honeysuckle is "too frondy", or my buddleia "too rampant", or a branch of my apple tree is overhanging the wall and invading his rotten garden and spoiling his "clean lines".

I thought, as I had a pretty good vantage point from the wall, that perhaps I could spot him and see what he's really like — and there's definitely a person-shape moving around by the house.

Honestly, this Man seems like an overprivileged idiot to me, and I'd quite like to see if I'm right about him.

'But is The Man even there today?' Fae's question is, I suppose, quite reasonable.

'Perhaps. But if I don't spy, I'll never find out, will I? There's definitely somebody around.'

'True.'

There's silence for a moment, broken only by the slobbering sound of Schubert licking up something unmentionable from the ground, and I lean over just a little bit further . . .

And then the silence is broken by me tumbling off the wall and squealing as I fall into a very overgrown border.

* * *

Marcus

The thing I love about driving back up here is looking forward to the peace and quiet. The unassuming predictability, I suppose, of the countryside around the house; the sound

4

of the birds tweeting — in fact, it's so peaceful, sometimes I think I can actually hear the grass growing.

Growing in my very overgrown garden.

It's something that I keep meaning to address; in fact, Carla said she'd look into it for me, but recently every time I come back, she seems to be doing something with the out-buildings, and the gardens look more and more sad. Carla likes to be known as my "Project Manager". And I suppose she is really, so I should give her the benefit of that title. She is contracted to work on my property, and she certainly thrives on the 'Manager' part of the position. I've known her for a while, and she's quite a determined, ambitious person.

She was a friend of my ex-girlfriend, Rachel. Rachel was a researcher on the first series of Hidden Architecture, the television show I present, when it had just started up. Rachel moved on to a different programme, a current affairs quiz show, before we began series two. At the time, Carla worked part-time on something called, InstaProof Your Pad, which was as dreadful as it sounds. It was a short-lived horror, presented by some awful Instagram influencer called Feenix Valdez, who, irrational as it sounds, I couldn't take seriously because of the way she chose to spell her name. Rachel and Carla were quite pally, and both of them were ambitious in their own ways. Rachel, because — I discovered later — she actually wanted to be part of a media power-couple; and Carla, because she wanted to break out of the buying-stuff-to-flaunt-on-Instagram game and design her own creations. She'd worked on a lot of programmes about home revamps, and had some background in the field. I knew she was capable — Rachel often told me how capable she was, in fact. I'd heard all about how Carla spent her spare time scouring auction houses and estate agents for "opportunities". To give her due praise, she has already successfully managed to update a couple of flats and a mid-terrace cottage using the contacts and the experience she's gained through her work in the media. So she knows her stuff.

5

Shortly after Rachel and I broke up, Carla began a fling with my friend Jonty, who works in production on Hidden Architecture. A group of colleagues came up for a visit one weekend and she pitched up as his plus-one. It's a small world, really. Anyway, Carla became very interested in what could be done with Glentavish and the potential it had. Her interest in Glentavish outlived her interest in Jonty, to be honest.

Glentavish House needed quite a lot of work doing to it when I first got it — probably something to do with it being a very old, very large house which has been battered by the Scottish weather for a good two hundred years or so. That weekend, Carla told me that InstaProof Your Pad had been binned after Feenix had slagged the team off in a drunken TikTok rant (did Feenix seriously think they wouldn't be monitoring all her social media?) — but it was apparently "all good", as Carla had decided she was ready for a new challenge anyway.

'I mean,' Carla had said, over a fish and chip supper for ten, 'this would be a great project to work on! InstaProof is over, I need something new to focus on, and you know I can do it, Marcus. I've done property development shows on TV, I've done it in real life. I know how it all works, and I can definitely stage interiors.'

So the upshot was that, after a few more discussions, I agreed to employ her as the Project Manager for the renovations. I was away too much to supervise things, and she was keen to take on the project. Basically, it was a win-win for both of us.

According to Carla, the outbuildings are a good place to focus on now the work has been done inside. Her favourite conversation, though, was repeated again last night when I called her to see how things were progressing and to let her know I'd be up today.

'Marcus, like I keep telling you, you need to futureproof this project,' she'd said. 'If you want to expand Glentavish House into a "brand" or a "business", everything has to have a high-end finish . . . and that's why we're overbudget on the kitchen appliances,' she'd added.

'Carla, I appreciate the thought, but let's not go there. You know what I really want right now is to come back to a home; not a brand or a business. I have enough "business" while I'm at work. I'm sure I won't be doing Hidden Architecture forever — and at some point, I will definitely be thinking about my future and how Glentavish can work for me — but for now, I want to actually just enjoy my home for a bit more than a weekend at a time.' It's true. All I really want is to chill out and enjoy the sunrises over the back lawn, and then nip to the village for a spot of shopping afterwards. 'And I understand what you're saying about the kitchen,' I'd continued, 'and I'm sure you kept it as close to budget as possible — but the only person I want to futureproof Glentavish for right at this moment is me.'

'Well, I'm very pleased with the kitchen,' she'd said in response to that.

Which was good, as it would be awful to work on something you hated, surely?

Carla also has a key to the property, which makes sense because I'm away working so much, so I won't be too surprised if she's there when I come back. I'm not really sure if Project Managers are supposed to live on-site or not, but she has claimed one of the spare bedrooms and seems to be around pretty much permanently. Even more so, since she broke up with Jonty. As you might have guessed, although Carla is completely confident in what she's doing, this is the only property development I've ever done, so I'm learning as I go. I'm more used to discovering previously hidden bits of — well — architecture, than living amongst the project.

Carla seems to thrive amongst the dust and debris, and I can't help thinking how Rachel would have hated the mess and upheaval of the renovation. Everything had to be perfect for her, which was quite possibly one of the reasons she broke up with me. I was definitely not the perfect boyfriend, by all accounts.

One of the reasons Rachel gave for ending it was because my schedule was (and still is) quite mad and I apparently put "too much energy" into my work — more energy than I put into my relationship, she told me. She didn't like the fact that I worked away so much, and that I didn't have a lot of time to spend with her. 'For God's sake,' she'd said in that final argument, 'I'm involved with Marcus Rainton from the Television, but nobody believes me because you're never around!'

I was rather stunned at that — not only because of the fact she made "Marcus Rainton from the Television" sound like my proper name, but because I'm just "me" at the end of the day. And "me" has to make hay while the sun shines — because I know that someday Hidden Architecture could be pulled from the schedules (but never because of a TikTok rant, obviously), and then all my appearances on chat shows, all the interviews, all the Sunday morning cookery shows and the odd (very odd) non-current-affairs quiz shows will fade into oblivion, and I'll just be plain old Marcus Rainton again. Not "Marcus Rainton from the Television".

The break-up also made me wonder if I even had time to think about relationships — it seemed maybe it would be just as unfair to whichever new woman I fell for. My time with Rachel had been fun to start with, but the cracks were showing in the distance between us, and we ended up realising we couldn't fill them.

So for now, it's simpler all round to be on my own and focus on my career.

However, all of this also means that I'm rarely able to get to Glentavish House at the moment, which is a shame. It's kind of in the back of my mind that I'll enjoy the place more "later on", and yes, maybe look at a commercial use for one of the outbuildings — but for now, my life is in London. "Later on" seems like a bit of a daydream, and I know I should be grateful that the work I do is so popular — at least for the minute.

I'm filming two new episodes of Hidden Architecture every week. Me hosting the show sort of happened by accident, if I'm honest. I've got a background in architecture, and a few years ago I made a discovery in someone's garden while I was working on a sun-room extension. It was a tunnel between what had been the old manor house and a local pub, which then led all the way to the sea — perfect for smugglers, and often referred to in local folklore, but never with any evidence to prove it . . . until I found it, of course. Local news crews had come to visit, followed by national news crews and other sorts of media — and for some reason, they liked me. I got the offer of the show, took it — because why wouldn't I want to do something so exciting? — and the rest is history.

The job, obviously, led me to Rachel, and then to Carla — and it was pretty obvious even at our first meeting that she was one to watch. She was soon leading the conversation and was very clear on the direction she wanted her career to travel in. However, even though I'm pretty easy-going in many ways, both in my personal and public life, I've found that there are some things Carla and I disagree on, time and time again. Like I say, she has a lot of ideas.

'This would be a perfect retreat centre,' she keeps saying. 'Can you imagine a group of yogis doing a sun salute at dawn on the east lawn? It's definitely something you could consider.'

The bit I haven't quite pinned down yet is where the yogis will retreat to when they aren't, well, yogi-ing.

Will they retreat to another outbuilding?

Will they retreat to the stable block?

Will the lawn turn into a campsite?

Or will they retreat back into the house itself?

It is this I am pondering as I continue my drive home.

CHAPTER TWO

Bea

'Cousin Bea?' Fae's voice carries over the wall.

'Mow wow?' Schubert adds his concerns to the proceedings.

'Bea Appleton?' Fae sounds curious rather than concerned.

'I'm the only Bea here, and I'm still alive, if that's what you're asking!' I shout back.

'That's okay then.'

'Mow wow.'

There is another short silence, then: 'Shall I summon help? Or is there a conveniently placed ladder or something you can scramble up?'

'There's no conveniently placed ladder.' I stand up and notice I've torn holes in the knees of my black tights, which is annoying. I stomp out of the border, brushing my bee outfit down. The fabric is oddly soft and furry, a bit like a proper bee, and it's strangely quite comforting to my fingertips as I follow the roundness of the costume with my strokes. 'No conveniently placed ladder at all.'

However, I can't escape the fact that I'm actually standing in the garden of the Big House, and a little thrill tingles its way from my toes right to the top of my head; I swear the deely-boppers tingle as well.

So this is it. This is the garden I've been banned from accessing, thanks to the way the properties have been divided. I suppose I am, technically, a trespasser at this very moment. The rebel in me laughs and laughs at that fact, and the gardener in me looks around to see if there's any evidence of the "clean lines" favoured by the owner.

There isn't.

Not from where I'm standing, anyway.

There is a tangle of sticky-jacks — sometimes known as "cleavers" or Galium aparine — which are universally fun for small children (or Fae) to throw at people and laugh as the long green stems stick to their clothing. I pull a few stalks off my outfit and toss them back into the mix, where they sink into a nest of ivy and bindweed, all matted together. I'm sure that somewhere a border is hiding, but I feel cross again at the fact my poor honeysuckle had to be chopped down when it dared straggle over the wall — when all along there was this on the other side.

'Do I deserve to be chopped down too? I'm invading your bloody garden after all,' I mutter, quite senselessly — but I am quite cross.

Beyond the border, there is a humungous, weed-ridden lawn, dotted with dandelions, daisies and clover, leading right up to the Big House. The house looks very impressive from ground level, and also rather intimidating now that I'm not peering at it from an eight-foot-high wall.

It's made from grey stone and looks as if, once upon a time, it was a very grand residence indeed. I can almost see ladies drifting around the lawn in their tea gowns or crinolines, or Bright Young Things wandering around in their tennis whites on a visit from London. There's an odd sort of stillness to the place, and I sense that, if I listened and looked hard enough, the images of the past residents would emerge and converge — with Lady Clementine presiding over them, hopefully — and I'd be just part of the story, woven into the fabric of the place; that in years to come, someone would turn and catch a glimpse of a woman with lilac hair and grass-green eyes, dressed as a bumble bee, tumbling out of the sky and landing in a pile of weeds . . .

I suddenly think that I see a white-clad figure standing in the big window that looks over the garden, but I squeeze my eyes shut and open them again, and of course there's nothing there. No Lady Clementine, unfortunately. Instead, I'm just looking at a beautiful old house with sun glinting off its windows; a house that looks far more welcoming now than I had first thought.

But the grounds. My word — the grounds! Beautiful as they are, they could do with a jolly good tidy-up. The lawn is impressive in its size, but weeds aside, it's straggling and looks like the last time it was cut was with a knife and fork after a particularly boozy lunch.

There is no way, no way on earth, that my honeysuckle — and my buddleia and my clematis and my rambling roses — should have ever been banned from this garden.

No way.

I put my hands on my hips and shake my head. I have no idea who The Man thinks he is, but a gardener he is not.

'Bea? Cousin Bea?' Fae's voice floats over the wall again. She's using a sort of stage-whisper, and it's quite amusing as there is nobody around who can hear except us.

'It's okay, Fae. I just need to find a way out. I'm fine.'

I stand for a moment longer in the overgrown border and look around. I suspect there must have been some way through to my garden at some point in the last two centuries, as my land was their walled garden after all. If only I could find Lady Clementine's mythical grand gateway!

'Mow wow.'

'Schubert thinks there should be a way through the wall,' calls Fae.

I swear she thinks they're being helpful, and they're really not.

'Yes, thank you. I know. I'm going to try and find it. Then I can come back that way, and hopefully The Man will never know I've been here.'

'Will it involve knocking old brickwork down, do you think? Will you need some sort of mallet? A big hammer we can use to knock the wall down? Because I'm not sure if we have a mallet in the garden, Bea!'

'Mow wow.'

Silence.

'Oh. My mistake. Watch out, Bea.'

I duck just in time as a mallet — an actual mallet — comes flying over the top of the wall and bounces on the grass next to me.

'Hey! Careful!' I jump away from the offending mallet and look at it as it lies there. Oh well. It can't hurt, can it? Well — it could hurt if it had landed on me, I amend silently, but for now I pick it up and start to prowl a bit. 'I'm sure there'll be an old rusted gate or something,' I shout back. 'There was supposed to be one, anyway, I think. Maybe I can find it and loosen the hinges with this mallet and we'll see what happens.' I start walking along the border. 'If I can't find any access, I'll just have walk back through the grounds.'

I know, I know, I'm dressed as a bumble bee. I'm going to look pretty weird pootling through the grounds like this, but what else can I do?

Like I say, I have no idea if there's still a gate between the two properties or not, but the border on my side is pretty rampant with climbing plants and ivy and the like, so if there is one, it could have been buried for years. I know from my research about Lady Clementine that one might have existed at some point, but who knows if it was ever built? It could even have been bricked up or demolished by now, eradicated by whatever they do to old gates they no longer want.

I continue cautiously along the border, wielding my mallet, peering at the wall as I go, just in case I spot a gate or two. To be honest, the plants on this side are so wild and entwined as well that I don't think I'm going to have much luck.

Eventually, there is a bit of the bindweed that looks extra knotted. I start probing at it — well, poking my black stockinged feet into the mass of greenery, and think I see something rusty in amongst it all. I take aim with my mallet, intending to gently nudge at it to see what happens, when I hear a screech from halfway across the garden.

'What are you doing in here?' yells a woman. I think I hear a hiss from the other side of the wall and deduce that Schubert mustn't like the tone of her voice. I don't particularly like it myself, but I suppose I do look a bit suspicious, dressed as a bumble bee, aiming a mallet at the wall.

'Get out! Get out!' the woman continues to yell.

So I stand where I am and watch her power towards me. She's wearing skin-tight jogging leggings and a skin-tight T-shirt. Her hair looks immaculate, pulled back from her face, but her skin is all taut at the sides where the tight ponytail is pulling.

As she gets closer, I see that the taut skin is nothing to do with a tight ponytail; it's more to do with the fact she's got a taut-looking face. Her lips are compressed in a mean little line and she's definitely scowling — as much as the tautness of her skin will allow, anyway.

I once heard someone say that when you hit forty, you have to choose between figure and face. This woman looks to be about my age, which is thirty-two, but she clearly has already made her mind up to choose "figure". I look at her and make the vow there and then that, in eight years' time, I will choose "face". Or at least I vow to try to keep smiling at people.

'I repeat, what are you doing in here?' she demands again.

I'm not prepared to yell back at her, especially not while I'm holding a mallet. I imagine I could be deemed quite intimidating if I did that. And yes, I may have lilac hair and be dressed as a bumble bee, but I do have my dignity.

I wait until she's almost upon me, and then say, quite calmly, 'I'm not prepared to yell back at you.' She looks shocked for a moment, especially when I lay the mallet down to prove I'm not actually a threat, as if she wasn't expecting me to respond in such a fashion; then she gathers herself together and sort of bristles before snapping:

'I don't care what you're prepared to do, or not prepared to do. I want you out of the garden. You're trespassing.'

'I'm fully aware I'm not in a public space.' I fold my arms across my round, fluffy, black-and-yellow tummy. 'And I'm actually trying to find my way out of here. But there doesn't seem to be an exit.'

'Just leave the same way you got in,' the woman hisses.

'I would need to scale an eight-foot wall in order to do that, then fall off the top. I'm not prepared to do that either. I'm looking for a gate between this garden,' I jab my finger towards the Big House, 'and that garden on the other side.' I jab my finger towards the wall. 'Hence the mallet. Believe me, I don't want to be in here a moment longer than I have to be.'

'Good. Because you're trespassing.'

'So you keep saying.' I'm trying to keep my temper, but this woman is rubbing me up the wrong way. 'If you could either direct me to a hitherto unknown access point where I can leave this garden and enter my own, I'd be most grateful.' I know I sound a bit formal here, but I'm trying to take the moral high-ground and, yes, I'm also trying to channel my old friend, Lady Clementine. I'm sure she wouldn't be intimidated by a woman dressed in Lycra.

'Your garden?' The woman's eyes widen, then narrow evilly. 'You're the one who has all that untidy stuff hanging over my wall?'

I'm thrown for a moment. I thought it was The Man who owned the Big House, not this woman. Or is it not A Man after all? I did, honestly think that A Man would be more inclined to take umbrage against fronds — and someone in the Post Office definitely referred to A Man buying the place.

'Your wall? Do you own this place?' I can't help but ask.

She looks shifty for a second. I know this because her eyes dart to the side, well, shiftily. Then she glares full-on at me, and I wonder if I was mistaken. 'My partner owns it, but I live here. And you need to leave before I call the police. Because you're trespassing.'

'All right, all right!' I mutter. 'Garden gate? Anywhere?' I jab my forefinger towards the wall again, but part of me already knows what the answer is going to be.

Sure enough, she compresses her lips nastily and folds her skinny arms across her flat little stomach. 'None. You have to go back the way you came, or walk out of the estate and find your own way back.'

She indicates a long driveway and I know it's my cue to walk towards it. It's a long time since I did a walk of shame whilst dressed so inappropriately.

It's incredibly annoying.

I try one last time. 'Do you perhaps have a ladder so I can go back over the wall?' The request almost chokes me, especially as she shakes her head slowly.

'No ladder.'

Right. Looks like I'm walking then. I don't bother dignifying her comment with a response.

'Bea?' Fae's little voice drifts over the wall again. 'Shall I try to chuck a ladder over the wall for you?'

Bless her.

'There are more of you?' The woman glares at me. 'There are no ladders coming over that wall from any direction, okay?'

'There is an entire horde of us,' I snap.

'Mow wow.'

'And a cat. A big cat. A massive, scary wild cat.'

'Mow wow!' Schubert makes his voice as massive and scary as he can. Bless him too.

'I hate cats,' growls the woman. 'They make a mess all over the garden. So you can get out, and your friends can keep out, and you can keep your cat out as well.'

There's an ominous silence from Schubert.

16

'The entire horde of us, and the feral cat as well, will all come back in the dead of night and scale the wall and . . . and — plant things.'

Okay, it wasn't the best comeback, which is why she looks at me so oddly, I guess, but it's all I have for now. I turn smartly on my black-stockinged heel. I've always wanted to turn smartly on my heel, and I think I did a fairly good job, all things considered.

'I'm walking, Fae,' I shout over my shoulder. I duck down quickly to collect my mallet before strutting off, nose in the air. 'Some woman won't let me find an exit in the wall.'

'Okay,' says Fae brightly. 'I'll pop the kettle on.' Which is just the sort of random thing my cousin would say to me.

There is still an ominous silence from Schubert, and even I can sense the shock and horror oozing silently — which is an odd statement, I know — from that mound of black fur over the wall at the fact this woman doesn't like cats.

'I know, Schubert. It's appalling, isn't it?' I hear Fae saying.

There is an even darker silence from Schubert.

'No sweetie, I don't think we can do a little hex on her,' says Fae.

This time, it's almost a charged silence from Schubert. But it doesn't seem to prevent Fae from understanding what he's saying. 'No, sweetie. Come on, let's get ready to welcome Bea back.'

I keep my head in the air and continue walking, even as Fae's voice gets fainter as she presumably walks towards the Visitors' Hut on the other side of the wall. I'm horribly aware of the woman's eyes on me. I'm sure she's got a mocking smile on those baby-pink lips as well, but I'm too angry to consider it further. I'm just focused on walking towards the long drive which winds away from the Big House, and thinking how awfully long it actually seems now I'm approaching it.

Eventually, I get out of her stupid estate by trudging down the longest drive in the absolute world, and find myself on the lane that leads to my Garden. I'm grumbling away to myself, feeling quite hot and sweaty, when I spot a car driving towards me. I manoeuvre myself into the hedgerow and keep walking, but the car slows down anyway and I catch a glimpse of a man driving it, staring at me in a sort of confused fascination.

Dignity. I must retain my dignity.

I do my best to ignore him — in fact, I channel Schubert's best supercilious look, trying to make it appear extremely reasonable that I'm walking down a country lane dressed as a bumble bee.

But I'll admit, I do have a second glance, because he's not exactly an ugly man, I have to say.

Far from it.

He's got fair hair and the sunlight glints in his eyes for a moment so they glitter hazel. He looks oddly familiar; like that chap from the television. The one that does Hidden Architecture, I say to myself. The chap from that goes around places and discovers secrets in outbuildings like cow sheds and outside loos, and always seems to know if a mansion used to be a cottage when it was first built. Marcus Rainton, I think he's called.

But then he's gone, driven past me towards his destination, and I'm still trudging along the lane dressed as a bumble bee.

My life is certainly never dull.

* * *

Marcus

I'm still pondering where the yogis will go, when I see a woman walking down the lane dressed as a bumble bee.

I've just finished a show where we explored a secret passage from a butler's pantry to the wine cellar, and speculated on butlers sneaking around to snaffle some homebrew, so I'm in quite a good mood anyway, despite all the stuff with Carla — and Ms Bumble Bee just makes me smile even more.

What a great costume! Even if she is swinging a mallet with every step. That's a little odd, to be fair.

I slow the car down to shout something encouraging out of the window when she gives me a filthy look and I think better of it. I decide it's best just to get back to Glentavish House and not shout encouraging comments to random women dressed as bumble bees.

I pull into the drive, clock a flapping piece of tarpaulin to my left and some scaffolding around an old outbuilding. Carla must have workmen in, but I've no idea what they're here for. I had asked her again if she'd see if we could get a landscape gardener in to sort the garden out, but I guess something else must have come up with the place as she's never mentioned gardeners since.

I park up in front of the house . . . and my heart sinks as I witness the emergence of an enraged Carla from the building.

She steps out of the door to wait for me. She's doing that thing where her hands are on her hips and she's tapping her foot. But I know she won't leave the doorway as she quite likes to stand there and preside over the place — her Project. She certainly has a sense of ownership over the development, which is a good thing, I guess.

'Marcus.' Her greeting is short and to the point, and, shockingly, rather like an angry squawk. Oh dear.

'Hello, Carla. Good to see you!' I smile at her as I get out of the car and hold my arms out to give her a friendly hug. I have to walk towards her with my arms outstretched though, as she definitely isn't going to move from the doorway.

'Marcus,' she says again, and offers herself briefly into my waiting hug before pulling away again and pointing somewhere in the vicinity of the wall at the end of the garden. 'Marcus, there was a trespasser. In the garden. In the actual garden, Marcus.'

Her eyes widen and she looks as if the idea of a trespasser in the garden is quite a big thing, which I suppose it is really.

I take my phone out of my pocket. 'Oh no. I'll ring the police. I'll—'

19

'No! There's no need for the police. I know who it was. It was a woman dressed as   a bumble bee.'

She looks so horrified and appalled, that I can't help bursting into laughter.

'A bumble bee? I think I saw her walking along the lane. Lilac hair? And a mallet?'

'Awful woman.' Carla shudders. 'And yes. That was her. Oh, she didn't try to hit me with the mallet or anything — but I was worried about property damage; she was edging very suspiciously along the garden wall. She said she thought there was a secret gateway in it or some such nonsense.'

'So do you know where she came from? What her intentions were? With the mallet, I mean? And the bumble bee costume?'

'Not really. She says she fell into the garden and mentioned something about owning that dreadful messy site on the other side of the wall. She says she was on top of the wall and was trying to find her way back out through this fictitious gateway — but perhaps she's just a stalker and a trespasser, and a weirdo. She's probably trying to throw herself at you, Marcus.'

'I doubt that. I'm not a rock star or a proper celebrity.' I laugh at the thought. Although according to Rachel, I am Marcus Rainton from the Television, so I might have more status than I originally realised. The idea is definitely amusing. I carry on. 'I present a show about old buildings. You know yourself it's hard work and not very glamorous. And nobody really knows I own this place anyway.'

'But old buildings are coming back into fashion,' Carla says. 'It's all about buying them, doing them up and selling them. It's about making them beautiful and modern inside. And all clean lines outside.'

When she first started officially project managing the renovation of Glentavish House and got a good look at the place, she recoiled at the layout inside. It's pretty higgledy-piggledy, even for a house of this age and size. I find the features charming and characterful, and love the fact there are nooks leading off corridors that end nowhere, or the small snatches of space beneath the eaves that are no good for any real purpose in this day and age, but boast real fireplaces in the corners, nevertheless.

Carla has, obviously, always been quite interested in buildings and interiors, because that was her job when I met her — but now she seems even more interested in how she can change them and modernise them. 'You can really do this place up,' she'd told me when she first visited, whilst waving a champagne cocktail expansively over the inglenook fire-place. 'I mean, some bifold doors instead of those old French doors into the garden room would be awesome. You could demolish that Victorian conservatory and extend outwards with floor-to-ceiling glass. Or you could knock down the walls between those three reception rooms along the side and have a huge kitchen-diner. I mean, nobody wants a library or a dreary old drawing room in this day and age.'

'I'm more interested in getting the Artex off the walls, restoring the oak floorboards and revealing original features, to be honest,' I'd said. 'And I want to install things like decent bathrooms, central heating and a useable kitchen.' But I'm not sure she was really listening to me at that point.

Carla is using Glentavish House as a step up the proper-ty-ladder for her career purposes and that's great. A lot of her ideas are good, but I sometimes think they're not necessarily in keeping with the ideas I personally have for Glentavish. I want to be more sympathetic towards Lady Clementine and Lord Archie Grey's vision for the place. They made it into a family home about a hundred and fifty years ago and I like that idea — I'm a little old-fashioned at times, I'll admit. So I have stopped her doing some of the more outlandish things she originally wanted to do, but there are definite "Carla" touches elsewhere — like in the aforementioned kitchen.

But I digress. The biggest bee in Carla's bonnet about Glentavish House is the wall between us and the neighbour-ing garden. She does genuinely — and unreasonably to me, because they're just Nature after all — hate the plants coming over to Glentavish's side and obsesses constantly over the fact that the boundary would look better with "clean lines". Every time I go away and return, another overhanging plant has vanished from the old stone wall, and it's starting to look a bit shivery and naked.

I've learned to pick my battles though, and I did live in fear for a bit that I'd come back to find out that she'd decided to block up one of the huge (working) fireplaces and replace it with a more fashionable log burner. She's enthusiastic, that's for sure.

I force my thoughts back to the mystery woman who'd apparently appeared in the garden.

I can't help smiling when I remember her stomping down the lane, then I see Carla's angry face and rearrange my smile into a serious expression. 'I suspect that there was a good reason for her to be on the wall,' I say, indicating that I'd quite like to enter the house.

It takes a moment and a couple more gestures from me before the penny finally drops and she moves.

'And if she's genuinely from next door, or it's a publicity stunt, I'm sure we'll find out soon enough,' I add.

'Hmmm.' Carla doesn't sound so sure, but as she follows me through the house, she gets sidetracked and starts telling me about Maxine Marling and her pet architect Paul Tanner. 'Paul has built Maxine a yoga studio. Imagine that.' Maxine Marling is a celebrity who, to my knowledge, Carla has never met, but she insists on talking about her as if they are actually friends.

'I suppose her ex-husband indirectly footed the bill again?' I was only asking out of politeness. I wasn't really interested in Maxine Marling, to be honest. She'd once been married to a footballer and was busy spending crazy amounts of her divorce settlement on crazy additions to her mansion in Islington — my flat is also in Islington, but my flat is not a mansion, I have no interest in Maxine's mansion, and, to be honest, Maxine Marling is a pain in the backside. She'd hooked Paul Tanner, a well-known architect, in the process of renovation, and for some weird reason Carla and Rachel follow their antics religiously. Maxine often sends her pet PA to hunt out my production team in order to offer her services, should we like to include her house on Hidden Architecture — but, to be honest, she's renovated the soul out of the old place, and that's not what my show is about.

I wonder afresh if Carla is aspiring to be like Maxine and go slightly crazy with the work on the house. Who knows? I've got a set budget for the work on Glentavish, which of course Carla can access, but I don't have unlimited football-er-style funds, so that might halt her plans if her aspiration is to make this place like her idol's.

'I don't know the cost but, like I say, I do know she has her own studio now. It was in Righty-O! magazine. I do quite fancy being a yoga instructor, actually . . .'

'Do you?'

'Yes. I've been looking at courses.'

'Okay. As well as doing your property projects?'

'I can do them both. And Eduardo says he can help me.'

Eduardo is Carla's yoga instructor. For someone who is only supposed to be here working on something, Carla has built herself quite a life in the nearby town.

'But don't worry. My priority is this project. I'll think about yoga in the future,' she adds quickly.

'Oh, that's entirely up to you — good luck if you can do it all. I couldn't help but notice that old outbuilding's got some scaffolding up, though?' I say, remembering that I saw some tarpaulin flapping in the breeze as I drove up to the house.

'It's needing a damp-proof course,' explains Carla, 'so I thought we might as well have it all sorted and cleaned up whilst they were in there anyway. Saves upheaval later. Did I tell you I've also been researching art retreats? Some of those look pretty good too. You know, once we've got the outbuildings sorted, there's a perfect opportunity there. I wouldn't mind working on moving that forwards.'

'Did you fancy doing an art retreat?' I ask, surprised. As far as I know, Carla can't even paint a wall, never mind a picture. She has "people" to do that for her.

'Oh no. I was just looking. Researching, like I said. Yoga's my preference. From what I gather, the art retreat property owners have to facilitate someone to come and run it. They just provide the space for the retreat.'

'Yes, yoga's more your thing, I guess. And anyway, you're not that fond of painting pictures and I'm not sure you really like being told what to do!' I grin at her, and she does almost smile.

'Who does like that? Anyway, I'd be the facilitator. A lot of these places have an artist in residence.'

'Where do they usually reside?' It is a genuine question, along the same lines as my retreating yogis pondering.

'They sometimes stay on-site.'

'And yogis. When they retreat, where do they go, exactly? Where do they retreat to? When they're not doing yoga?' Like I say, it's a question that I've been thinking about.

'Marcus!' She rolls her eyes. 'You're just being difficult now. Rachel said your sense of humour was warped.' Ouch. 'The yogis live on-site too, for the period of the retreat. They come to get away from the pressures of real life.'

I nod towards the flapping tarpaulin. 'So what you're saying is that you think you could get people retreating up here?' I say it jokingly, but her now serious expression tells me that she maybe hasn't taken it as a joke.

'Honestly, Marcus! This place is perfect for an enterprise like that. If you let me use the buildings, I could make some money in an instant by organising a retreat. You should let me. It would be great exposure. For us both. I need to future-proof myself as well, you know?'

'Well, maybe at some point,' I say, just to close the conversation down. 'But I certainly don't want you to do anything imminently.'

'Noted.' She nods quickly. 'Okay. I shall be in my office if you need me.'

She turns sharply into a room which was, according to the old plans, the original study, and shuts the door firmly.

I'm left standing in the hallway, feeling like I haven't really come back to my very own house after a whole fortnight away in my London flat, but instead that I've stumbled into some sort of corporate world. Since when did Carla have an office in Glentavish House? I mean she has to work somewhere, I guess — but it's a bit weird hearing her refer to the study as her office. I've never really thought about it before . . .

I also feel rather confused about the conversation we just had.

And, rerunning the conversation in my head, I actually do feel a little frisson of unease. What did she mean by "noted"? Then I shake my head.

Hey, this is me, and I'm more than likely overthinking things.

CHAPTER THREE

Bea

'Bea. Cousin Bea. I've got the merchandise.'

'Mow wow.'

It's been two weeks or so since I fell into The Man's garden, and I'm only just getting over the humiliation of it. It'll take me longer to get over the anger I have for that awful woman who I encountered, though. I look up from the desk in the Visitors' Hut to see Fae bearing down on me with an enormous trunk.

A trunk!

If she'd brought the merchandise — what merchandise, actually? — in a bag or a briefcase, that just wouldn't be Fae. So to see her with a Victorian travelling trunk makes me hide a smile.

The trunk is balanced on a tartan shopping trolley, apparently so she can transport it more easily.

Regally reclining on the top of the trunk is Schubert.

I don't ask.

But she tells me anyway as I watch, fascinated, while this enormous black cat slithers off the trolley and pools into a seemingly even more enormous pile of black fur on the ground.

'It was easier to transport it this way,' she tells me. 'And Schubert fancied a ride.'

'Okay . . . But couldn't the merchandise—' again what merchandise? '—have gone inside the shopping trolley, rather than on the top of the shopping trolley? In a Victorian trunk?'

Fae pauses for a moment and looks thoughtful. 'Well, yes, Bea, I suppose it could have.' I can almost see her acknowledge the thought, then let go of it; then she shrugs her shoulders to dismiss it. I understand that the discussion is over on that matter.

'Hello, Schubert,' I say instead, turning my attention to the cat. He is staring at me and I can sense he needs acknowledgment.

'Mow wow,' he repeats.

'Can I ask why Schubert decided to come?' I address Fae.

Fae looks at me strangely. 'Because he wanted to.'

'And are you . . . looking after him again today?'

Fae looks at the cat and he looks back at her.

'Yes, Bea. I am. Well — to be precise, he said he wanted to come here, and I was coming, so it was kind of . . . organic. Anyway. The leaflets look amazing.'

She plunges her hand into the trunk and scrabbles around for a moment.

'Oh! You've brought the leaflets. When you said merchandise, I wasn't quite sure what—'

Bea plops a pile of labels advertising Bea's Bees Honey down, starring me dressed as a bee on the wall — which I wasn't bargaining on, but they do look pretty good. Then she brings out a sheaf of postcards and puts them down, and then she brings out the advertising leaflets which are the only things I was sort of expecting her to organise. I should have known when she mentioned "merchandise" it would be more than just leaflets, I suppose.

'Hang on!' I pick up a postcard. On the front are four pictures, and in the middle of them is my "Bea's Garden" logo. The top left picture is me dressed as a bumble bee; top right is a photograph of the Meadow Garden; bottom left is a picture of our Water Garden — and bottom right is Schubert sitting amongst my beehives. 'Schubert's on here?'

'Oh — yes. He's contemplating the beehives and looking quizzical. See?' She jabs the photo with forefinger and smiles indulgently. 'What a cutie. Aren't you a cutie, Schubert?'

'Mow wow.' The cat sounds smug and I blink, wondering which parallel universe version of Bea's Garden I've suddenly been launched into here. Schubert is nothing to do with my Garden. He's my cousin's boyfriend's sister's cat, and yes, he visits frequently, but I didn't have him down as a—

'—mascot. Yes, I know, Bea, but he's a USP. As well as the honey, of course.' Fae frowns, even as I'm taken aback by her knowing what I'm thinking. I hate it when she does that. Then her face clouds over a little. 'Having said that, I don't think you can have two USPs can you, Bea? A Unique Selling Point is unique, so by default you should only be advertising one. That's fine.' She smiles at Schubert. 'Loads of people sell honey, so yes, Schubert is your USP mascot. Good boy, Schubert. Good boy.'

'Mow wow.' The cat is definitely proud of himself.

'Anyway,' Fae continues. 'Isabel helped with the technical side of the merchandise. She's good, isn't she?'

Isabel is Alfie's teenage niece; the daughter of Scott, one of his brothers.

'Yes.' I nod. Isabel has certainly done a good job with the photos. 'Do you think—?'

'Her mum will put some leaflets in Belle and Scamp for you? I've already asked her, and yes she will.'

'Okay. Thanks. You'll have to—'

'Thank her. Yes, I will. Oh, and Billy is going to hand some out to the people who go on his ghost tours.' Billy is another of Alfie's brothers. He runs ghost tours in local cemeteries, and he met his partner, Lexie, when she attended one of his events.

28

You've actually just got to go with Fae's quirks at responding to questions you haven't even asked yet. But I do know Belle and Scamp, which Isa's mum, Liza ("rhymes with Tizer," as she keeps telling everyone) owns, is one of the finest vintage upcycling shops in Edinburgh with a lovely tea room on the first floor — so it'll be super to get some information in there and attract a few more people to my Garden.

'Yes, and I've already dropped some off at some of the other cafés and tea rooms in the area, so we're well covered,' adds Fae.

I simply nod.

'So I think when you do your Honey Festival, it'll all look pretty good, won't it?' Fae looks up at me and smiles.

My Honey Festival probably sounds grander than it is. It'll actually just be a few tables and things out on the meadow area with pots of honey from my bees, and bits and bobs that go well with it — lotions and potions made from plants in the garden, a few relevant snacks like honey cakes and honey ice-creams and herbal infusion teas, as well as normal tea and coffee. This will be the fourth Honey Festival I've done now, and I have my trusty list of stallholders, as well as my trusty list of lessons learned over the years reminding me that some things work (my friend Pippa's Coffee Van) and some things don't (a small bouncy castle, which we couldn't get Isabel and Nessa off of, and which Schubert stuck his claws through when he tried to join in).

There's also free herbalist advice at the Festival from Fae, who works out of her Apothecary's Cart. The cart is a revamped Gypsy caravan that lives on my premises, and Fae brings her horse, Roger, along for the event. Roger stands next to the caravan and smiles at everyone — although, one of the things that doesn't work at Honey Festivals is having Roger too close to greenery, as he enjoys a tasty snack far too often for the health of my Garden, basically eating anything he can reach.

Fae is a pharmacist in her real job, and she's like a completely different person when she's behind the counter at work doling out prescriptions and medicines; here, she's like an ethereal being who sort of floats around communing with Nature and totally "seeming at one with the place" — just like I feel here.

The Garden loves her and understands her, and I know that for a fact. It's surprising what the Garden tells you if you just sit and listen.

I just wish it would tell me where the gate is in that wall.

'So do you like the Honey Festival leaflets, Cousin Bea? Do you? You do, don't you?' Fae smiles serenely and puts another pile of flyers on the desk, bringing me back to the situation at hand. 'Schubert says he's definitely coming to that one. He's already told the bees.' I bet he has, I think, casting a glance at the cat. Probably when he was contemplating and looking quizzical—

'Mow wow.'

'Yes — that's right. He says that's exactly what happened,' says Fae, like it's a completely normal thing that she now seems to be reading a cat's mind.

It probably is, knowing Fae.

Regardless of what Schubert has or hasn't told my bees, she nods over to the Big House. 'You should invite The Man as well — let him see what it's like here. Then he might understand you and the Garden better.'

'Nope. The Man hates me.'

'Do you know that for sure? Has he actually said, "I hate you, Bea Appleton"?'

'No. He's never said "I hate you, Bea Appleton". Not to my face, anyway.'

I realise that he's never seen my face, anyway.

'Well then, he doesn't necessarily hate you.'

'He wants clean lines.'

'That doesn't preclude him from enjoying your Honey Festival . . . or not hating you.'

'Hmmm. His girlfriend yelled at me and said I was trespassing.'

'You don't know that it was his girlfriend.'

30

'Okay. Partner.' I make little bunny ears around the word "partner" and pull a face.

Fae ignores me. 'He hasn't said you were trespassing, though.' She fumbles around a little more. She pulls out another leaflet. I see that it's a list of cakes and baked goods. 'Tavey's Whisk and Waffle group,' she explains. Octavia is her brother Fergus' fiancée — and by default, my cousin Fergus' fiancée, I guess. 'Price list. Tavey says they'll bring fancy china along too, and a marquee, so visitors can enjoy tea and cake.'

'Mow wow?'

'No sweetie, not fishcakes.'

'That's kind of Tavey,' I comment.

'Mow wow?'

This time, I find I am drawn to look at the cat. He looks sad.

'Will he have some tuna?' I find myself asking, although he's the furthest thing from a starving beast I've ever seen. 'Means as he won't get fishcakes?'

'Mow wow?' He looks up at me hopefully, and two eyes glitter hungrily. I'm entranced by his gaze and find myself reaching over to my lunchbox and tossing him the tuna sandwich I'd brought for lunch.

'Mow wow.'

'You're welcome,' I respond, and watch as his jaws chomp down on my sandwich as he drags it outside somewhere to hoover up.

'Okey dokey then,' says Fae and suddenly pauses, turning to face outside and lifting her face to the sky. 'Time for me to go, I suspect . . . Ah-ha!' She points to the tartan shopping trolley and turns back to face me, then smiles one of her lovely smiles. In unison, we both look at the trolley and it rings. Well, the mobile phone she obviously has stashed inside it rings.

Fae's sixth sense is clearly working today. She rarely brings her phone out, which can be irritating if you're trying to contact her.

I watch her rummage in the trolley, and wonder if her phone is the only thing in there. Eventually, she brings it out and answers the call. She chats away to someone and I gather it's work.

'Yes, yes, that's no problem. I can come in straight away. What did they eat? Oh, I wouldn't go there for my mid-morning snack. What were they thinking—?'

The conversation continues for a few moments, and I can glean that her colleagues have had some dodgy sausage sandwiches and are now quite ill as a result, so Fae has been called in on her day off.

'All right, Cousin Bea. I'll see you another day then,' she says cheerfully once she's hung up and carefully replaced the phone back into the depths of the trolley. She leans over to kiss me. 'Bye bye! You can hang onto the trunk, but I need the tartan trolley.'

She heads out of the Visitors' Hut and starts tugging the trolley along behind her. I suddenly remember and shout after her: 'But wait! What about Schubert?'

'Oh, you can keep him too,' she says blithely over her shoulder. 'Someone will be along to collect him presently. He said he was going to stay here and be helpful for a bit. And he's had some lunch now, so he'll probably just have a short nap.'

'But who's coming for him?' I cry.

'Someone,' she says. 'Someone will come.' And she disappears out of view.

Then a single bee buzzes through the door. I smile at it — I think I know which one it is — and I hold my hand out. The bee (it's Bertie, I was right) comes and sits in my palm. I raise my hand so my eyes are level with his and I blow him a little kiss.

'I know,' I tell him. 'It's a bit odd, isn't it? What am I going to do with a cat? I'm not used to cats — although I do like them.' He buzzes in response and turns himself around like a dog getting itself comfy before it flops into a heap for a doze. 'Yes. I suppose you're right. I guess we'll just have to wait and see who turns up for him. I have no choice but to believe her, do I?'

Bertie buzzes his agreement and I tilt my hand gently, moving it so he slides off onto a posy of wildflowers. They're in a jam jar, specifically for this purpose, and I know which ones are his favourites. My little bee-friend nestles into the centre of a buttercup, and, bathed in the golden light from the petals, he snuggles down and pops his head between his front legs, folding his wings up neatly.

I watch him for a moment and then look outside the door. There's a heap of Cat just in view, also nestled in a patch of buttercups. The reflected yellow of those petals stripes his black fur with sunbeams and he looks a little bee-like himself. I study him for a moment, wondering how he would look dressed in a sweet little bumble bee outfit, and he opens one eye and stares at me. I can tell he's opened one eye because it's glinting in the black fur.

'Okay,' I hear myself say. 'I won't dress you as a bumble bee.'

'Mow wow,' he mutters. The eye closes and he begins to snore.

* * *

Marcus

I've never been to the Garden on the other side of the wall. It's one of those things where, because it's so close to your house, you just sort of take it for granted.

I bought Glentavish House from a company called Hogarth Properties, and it was quite clear in the deeds that the piece of land on the other side of the wall had become, over the years, a separate entity. I decide that today is the day that I'll go and visit it. There's no time like the present, as they say, and Carla has popped into town to attend a yoga class so I'm not needed to bounce any ideas off.

She doesn't usually need me for that anyway.

It's been a couple of weeks since I encountered the woman dressed as a bee walking down the lane, and I've found it difficult to get her out of my mind. This week, I was on the south-east coast, looking at the remains of a World War Two bunker, and there were some beehives on the dunes. They made me think of the human bee and that made me smile.

So today I find myself wandering down to the bottom end of the garden, coffee cup in hand, sunglasses on, staring up at the wall. The border on my side is embarrassing to say the least — never mind the secret gateway into the Garden on the other side which Carla mentioned, the border could potentially be hiding a lost tribe.

As it is, I already feel as if I'm being watched intently somehow.

I shiver a little uncomfortably and decide that it can't be any worse on the other side — and, with the obvious lack of a visible gateway between the two gardens, there is nothing for it but to walk back towards the house, back along the lane, and pitch up as a paying visitor.

It seems a convoluted way of getting there, and I smile again as I recall the girl with lilac hair I saw trudging down the side of the road. I wonder if she'll be the one taking entry fees today. I don't normally come up here fortnightly. I don't come up much at all, and on a day like today, where it's bright and sunny and beautiful, I wonder again why I don't make more of an effort.

I have no answer, beyond "work".

Maybe Rachel had a point.

But there's only one way to find out if Bee-girl is on the counter today; so I drain my coffee, take my empty cup back to the house and start the trek to the Garden.

A while later, I walk in through the entrance gate and stand, mesmerised, in the middle of the pathway leading to the Visitors' Hut. I inhale the scent of early summer; dug earth and sun-warmed herbs and cut grass and so many fresh, citrusy fragrances mingling with the last delicious notes of spring. Everywhere I look are pathways and little signs telling me to head to the Croft Garden, or the Jacobite Garden, or the Monastery Garden, or the Apothecary's Garden. Hidden amongst the plants are ornaments and statues and precious stones; everything perfectly complementing the contents of the Garden.

I let my gaze rove around the area, and, because of my work and my knowledge of these places, I can see, just faintly, where old meets new; where flower beds have been repurposed; where pathways have been merged or cut into over the years; where hedges have been trained to grow and subsequently gone rogue . . .

But it works. It really works and the buzz of entranced visitors — and the actual buzz of bees as they go to work on the flowers — makes my heart lift. Why haven't I come here before?

I suspect this side of the garden wall is just as chaotic as my side, but this is chaotic with a purpose. Not just chaotic and a mess.

I follow the path to the wooden Visitors' Hut and smile as a big, fat black cat stares into the lily pond next to the Hut and delicately sticks the tip of its tongue into the water. I don't think I'd want to drink out of the pond — I'd have thought the water might be a little stagnant — but further around I can see a big, shiny ball, brimming with water that bubbles and runs into the pond, presumably by means of a pump. So maybe it's not that stagnant — although I still don't think I'd like to drink out of it.

'It's perfectly clean.' The voice surprises me and I look around to see the girl with lilac hair studying me. She's wearing wellington boots, frayed denim shorts and a black T-shirt, and she's hugging a trug to her body with a trowel, a fork and a pair of secateurs sticking out of the top. Her hair is tied up with a rainbow-coloured scarf and she is watching me through eyes that are somewhere between the green of the grass at my feet and the shiny, dark leaves of one of the plants nearby. 'Its source is an ancient spring, and there's a constant flow of water to it, helped along by the ball fountain.' She nods at the cat. 'That's why he likes it. He says it tastes fresher—' She pauses and looks bemused, then puts her head on one side, as if she's just realised she's given the cat a voice. 'Anyway. Yes. Spring water—'

'Mow-ubble-ubble wow-ubble-ubble,' The cat mutters, I presume, a watery rejoinder; but as his nose is now in the water too, it sounds like he's blowing bubbles through a straw into a glass of lemonade.

'Sacred spring water. Apparently.' The girl smiles fleetingly at the cat and shakes her head. 'That's Schubert. I'm looking after him until someone can pick him up. He's no bother. Would you like to visit the Garden?'

'Um, yes. Please. That's kind of my intention.'

'Lovely. Come on then, I'll get you a ticket.'

I follow her into the Hut and spot a hand-painted sign nearby that says: No dogs allowed. They could eat something unsavoury and die. Beneath that is an addition scrawled in blue crayon: cats can bee hear.

The girl with lilac hair catches me looking at it and smiles. 'My cousin's partner's niece, Maggie May McCreadie, had a hand in that. Don't ask.'

I smile back. 'That's a good name for an artist. I assume the black cat outside has special dispensation then?'

'You assume correctly.' Then she rings a ticket through the till and I hand her the cash.

The girl points at a neat pile of maps. 'I suggest you take one of those if it's your first visit. It'll help you get your bearings.'

'Thanks.' I pick one up and study it, looking at the hand-drawn interpretation of the site, and trace what looks like a reasonable route through the Garden with my fingertip. 'I've never been here before, so this is great.'

'Have you come far?'

'Ummm, no. No. Not far.' Yes, I know it's a lie, but seeing this side of the wall has made me totally ashamed of my side, and if this girl thinks I live there and I've never even come here, then it's not making a very good first impression, is it?

36

The girl studies me and I feel myself flush. 'I know you. I do! Didn't I see you driving up the lane the other week?' The sunny expression suddenly turns into a scowl. 'I was dressed as a bee! You drove past me!'

'Yes — yes, that's right.' I sense myself wanting to defend my actions so she doesn't think I was just staring at her when I drove past. 'I was going to say something uplifting to you, but I decided I'd best not. You didn't seem as if you wanted to be uplifted.'

'I wasn't in the mood to be uplifted. If you'd found me half an hour earlier, I would have loved to have been uplifted. I was stuck on the other side of that wall being yelled at by a skinny woman with an attitude. I needed a crane to lift me back over this side — but you know, she wouldn't even get me a ladder? I suspect she's something to do with The Man.' The girl nods decisively.

The Man?

'The Man?' I ask.

'Yes. He owns Glentavish House and he keeps sending me nasty notes telling me to cut my plants down as they're encroaching and — oh!' She points at me and her eyes widen. 'Marcus. Marcus Rainton. That's who you remind me of. I bet you get that all the time, do you?'

'Constantly.' I smile, almost apologetically. 'That's because I am Marcus Rainton.' I take my sunglasses off and hold my hand out to her. A sixth sense tells me not to reveal I own Glentavish House just yet. The woman seems nice — even though she doesn't seem to rate Carla much. I have to say, I do find Carla's actions a little difficult to defend in this case. She could have helped this woman get back over the wall instead of making her do such a humiliating walk of shame on a public road.

'Really? You're Marcus Rainton? I did wonder.' She nods towards the sunglasses. I realise they're not a very good disguise, so it's good that I didn't really intend to arrive incognito. Like I say, I don't think of myself as Marcus Rainton from The Television, and so don't normally feel I need to hide my identity. I'm clearly rubbish at disguises, so that's probably a good thing. 'I'm very pleased to meet you then,' the woman continues. 'I love your show. I keep wondering if anything exciting is hidden here.' Her face changes for a second and she scowls again. 'I don't know, like a gate between the properties or something. Oh well.' Then her smile is suddenly back and she holds her hand out to shake mine. 'Bea. Bea Appleton. I own this place. So welcome to my Garden. Are you just passing?'

'Umm.' I think quickly. 'Sort of. I'm just here for a little while. Visiting.'

'Visiting? That's nice.'

'It's a mess on the other side of that wall,' I offer, and her eyes widen again.

'Have you been into that garden? Are you doing a show about it? Might we find a gate after all?'

'Oh, um, I'm not doing a show exactly. The Man you mention. He's, umm . . .' How can I say this?

'You're visiting The Man?' Bea's voice rises an octave and she looks a bit scary. What is it about Bea? I'm used to standing up for myself, but I'm just not the sort of person to send notes telling others to cut their plants down. I don't know enough about plants for a start. Plus it's just horrible and not very neighbourly.

'Yes,' I hear myself say pathetically. 'I'm visiting The Man. He's my cousin.' I smile at her in a hopefully charming way, and decide it's best I leave the Visitors' Hut before things get any more awkward in here. 'This way, is it? Right. I'll have a look then. Thanks again!' And I scurry out of there as fast as I can.

The conversation about my ownership of Glentavish House is, I decide, a conversation for another day.

Outside, however, I almost fall over Schubert the Black Cat.

'Mow wow,' he says, and I swear there's a challenge in his tone.

But he's a cat and I'm a human, and that's just daft.

CHAPTER FOUR

Bea

I watch Marcus Rainton wander out into the Garden and fold my arms. He seems . . . normal. Not like a celebrity. I've never really thought about what Marcus Rainton would be like in real life, though. But I've watched him on the TV show smiling at the camera and chatting to the owners of all these stately piles and little country cottages. He's typically good-looking; fair hair, warm eyes that are more brown than hazel when the sun isn't glinting in them, and the sort of chiselled bone structure that should be moodily advertising expensive aftershave on a beach at sunset.

And how bizarre that his cousin lives next door! That blonde woman must be something to do with the cousin. She did say her partner owned the place.

Hideous people.

I wonder if the Garden makes a good impression on Marcus Rainton, whether he'll be able to influence The Man? I mean, all I want is for my plants to be allowed to grow as Nature intended and not be hacked back all the time. But if he could find a doorway or gateway, then that would be absolutely super-cool, and—

'Mow wow!' Schubert starts to get over-excited. I can only tell this is happening because his voice goes up an octave and he starts prancing on his paws. I have a feeling that he feels he is elegantly prancing in a gloriously cheerful and light-hearted way, but the reality is he's stomping heavily with a serene expression on his face.

So long as he's happy, I guess.

'Is someone coming for you then, Schubert?' I ask him. He's also looking a bit like one of those Pointer dogs when they spy something, and he's straining to see into the car park whilst still prancing.

It's the oddest sight.

'Mow wow,' he responds and bounces a couple more times.

I follow his gaze and I see Nessa, his owner, walking purposefully towards us. No wonder Schubert is excited. He's devoted to Nessa and she's devoted to him. Nessa is Alfie's twin sister. And Alfie, if you recall, is Fae's boyfriend. I've known Nessa for a little while; she works for someone called Mr Hogarth — in fact, Hogarth Properties was the company who sold the Garden to me.

Bertie buzzes past me as I watch Nessa come towards us. He circles my head in a friendly way and zig-zags off towards her. He's a good judge of character is Bertie. He pauses in front of Nessa and hovers there for a moment. Nessa stops and holds her hand out, palm upwards, much as I did earlier, and Bertie lands on it. She leans in towards him and whispers something, and after a moment he bounces a bit, then zooms off to his hive and his friends.

I smile and wave at Nessa as she comes towards me.

'Telling it to the bees, are you?' I ask her.

'Well, of course!' She grins, and then crouches down and opens her arms, and Schubert galumphs towards her. Somewhere, a Richter Scale is breached.

'Oh, he's such a good boy, he's such a handsome boy. Did Mummy miss her boy? I think she did miss her boy,' says Nessa, rubbing her face in his fur. I can't help but recoil a little.

I'm not sure if she knows where that fur's been. It's certainly been into everything in the Garden, including the compost heap as I saw him standing on it earlier. It amused me at the time, as it looked as if he was trying to peer over the wall into The Man's garden, almost as if he was waiting for someone to appear, or maybe he was just studying the lay of the land.

'He was in the compost heap earlier,' I tell Nessa. I feel it's only fair to warn her.

'Is that going to make my lickle kitty cat grow into a big kitty cat then?' she asks, rubbing the soft bits behind his ears, which makes him go into ecstasies.

He's huge anyway, so I have no idea how much bigger Nessa thinks he can actually get. I'd have thought a more appropriate response to the news that her pet has been in the compost heap would be "oh no, and that has to come in my car!" But he won't be getting into my car, so it's not my problem.

'It had fresh horse manure in it as well,' I continue conversationally. Fae's horse, Roger, is quite good at providing that for us. 'The compost heap, you know?'

'Lovely for the roses,' says Nessa and stands up, apparently not bothered in the slightest that Schubert has been squelching through horse poo and will soon be squelching into her car. 'Thank you for looking after him.'

'I didn't really have much choice, but he wasn't any bother. Fae had to unexpectedly dash off to work.'

'Hmmm.' Nessa nods. 'I thought as much. Have you had any interesting visitors today?'

'Mow wow! Mow wow!' shouts Schubert, suddenly very over-excited.

Nessa looks at him then widens her eyes. 'Oh! Marcus Rainton? Gosh. Does he live nearby?'

'He's visiting his cousin,' I tell her. I jab my finger towards the Big House. 'Over there.' I don't question the fact Schubert has apparently told her this nugget of information. Nessa and Schubert have always seemed very much attuned to one another.

41

'Oh. I thought he'd actually bought a place up here. Mr Hogarth—'

'Mow wow! Mow wow!'

'Really? My goodness.' Nessa considers Schubert for a moment then looks at me. 'He says he saw Marcus Rainton in the garden before. When he was in the compost heap. Schubert was in the compost heap, that is. Not Marcus Rainton. He seemed to be very at home—'

'Mow wow.'

'Marcus Rainton, that is. Not Schubert. Schubert says he wouldn't like to live in the compost heap or be at home in one.'

'Mow wow.'

'He says he was looking curiously at the wall. Marcus Rainton was looking. Not Schubert.'

'Okay!' I say brightly before this gets any more surreal. 'Thank you. And thank you, Schubert, for your observations. Yes. Marcus Rainton is wandering somewhere in the Garden. He just came a few moments ago. I'm hoping he sees how nice this side of the wall is, compared to his cousin's side. Have you got everything for Schubert?' Having said that, I don't think he had anything with him when Fae brought him. Not even Catnip.

Catnip is Schubert's toy mouse. It's icky and smelly, but he seems to love it and is rarely without it. The person who is looking after him normally has Catnip around their personage somewhere, "just in case", Nessa insists. Nobody is sure what possession of Catnip might mitigate "just in case", but people seem to obey.

'No, Catnip decided to stay at home today,' says Nessa, picking up Schubert. How she doesn't overbalance, I have no idea, because she's not very tall and Schubert is substantial. 'So that's a very good reason to get this little man home as well. Thanks again.' She smiles at me and turns to leave. 'I'm sure you'll be seeing a lot more of Marcus Rainton. Mark my words.' And then she vanishes around the corner, and

I'm left with that weird, itchy feeling that Nessa's confident declarations sometimes give me.

I've discovered she's rarely wrong, so I'm just wondering what she means by that one when Marcus Rainton appears from behind the hedging, following the map carefully. I watch him as he pauses and looks up towards the wall, then down to the stones that form the small barrier between the border and pathway. Then he looks up again, and walks a few steps towards the wall. Then, to my surprise, he climbs into the border, pauses again, and pushes his way through the honeysuckle and the jasmine and the wisteria until he's almost hidden from sight.

'Hey!' I shout, beginning to jog over, unreasonably miffed. 'Hey! Where are you going? I'd thank you not to walk in my borders, if you can possibly help it. There are pathways to follow that will give you a better overview of the Garden!'

'Yes,' comes his voice from behind the foliage. 'But none of those pathways will take me through to the garden next door, will they? But this one might!'

'What? A pathway? In there?' I follow him and push through into the canopy of flowers and it's such a weird feeling. You might imagine what it's like if you were behind a waterfall, pressed against a rock face with a sheet of water thundering down in front of your face.

This is akin to that. Only I'm pressed against an uneven stone wall, and it's warm and snug and I'm surrounded by dapples of green and white — but it seems to be quite a large space. It's absolutely surreal. I feel like I'm in a floral cave as the flowers gently close in on us, leaving us standing in a sort of secret garden. The scent is amazing and I get shivers down my spine as I turn around 360 degrees and see the stems of the plants all intertwined, leaving just enough space for Marcus and myself to stand beside one another in a sort of bower, as a blossoming version of a waterfall hangs around us. It's nearly silent, and it almost feels as if we are removed from the world in here. Bees buzz nearby and I have the sense

43

of being completely at home. I know the bees won't harm us and I'm overwhelmed, actually, by just how beautiful it is in this hidden space.

These plants were here when I bought the garden. They're old and magical and very, very picturesque. I've never wanted to interfere with them. Why would I?

And this, this is what they've been secretly protecting, all these years.

I had no idea.

And yes, there is a gate in the wall. In fact, there's a huge set of double wrought iron gates, so densely covered in climbing plants that you'd never see them from the Garden. You'd never see them unless you came behind this flowery cascade.

'How did you find it?' I ask. My voice is almost a whisper, so keen am I not to break whatever spell I feel I'm under.

'The edging stones,' Marcus replies. His voice is almost a whisper too. I chance a look up at him, and he looks down at me, a tinge of excitement in his eyes. 'I saw that a few looked different — like they'd been added to fill up a gap. The gap was the path to this gate. They've kind of connected the two sides of your flowerbed, filled the soil up, and completed it by adding some extra edging stones. They're quite weathered, so it was done years ago, but they were less weathered than the rest.' He smiles. 'Also, I was looking at the map you gave me, and I could see the shape of the old garden laid out sort of underneath this one, so I worked out where the symmetries were — and I pushed through to find this.' He lifts his hand and indicates the gates. 'I don't suppose they've been opened in decades.' He touches the ironwork tentatively, and I half expect his hand to go through the rusty pattern, but it doesn't. 'I'll have to work out where it is on the other side,' he muses.

'I'd hazard a guess at that bit covered in bindweed and sticky jacks. I was heading that way when that woman chased me off the property. If you hack all the weeds away — or your cousin hacks it all away, whatever — you'll probably manage to open it out from his side too. I wonder where the key is? It's got to be in the Big House somewhere, hasn't it? If they owned the garden, I suspect the gates were locked up on their side when they separated the two parts of the estate. I certainly haven't come across it. But hey! What a find! Thank you so much.' I hold my hand out to shake Marcus', and as he takes mine to shake it back, a bolt of electricity shoots up my arm and I gasp.

The surge must have been felt by the bees nearby, as they rise and form a small swarm, then, just as quickly, settle back into their flowers.

'Bees,' says Marcus. He looks a bit wary. He also, I notice, folds his arms in front of his body.

I do the same.

'They won't harm us,' I reassure him. 'They're just as excited as I am — although I must ask Bertie why he never thought to tell me this was here.'

'Bertie?'

'My pet bee. Oh look! There's like a cat-flap at the bottom.' I laugh and point at a smaller gate, built into the big one. 'Schubert would love that — in fact, it would be absolutely ideal, because he could sneak in and rampage and upset that mean girl on the other side . . . oops. Sorry. I suspect she's something to do with your cousin.' I feel my cheeks heat up.

'Carla?'

'No idea — is that the mean girl who doesn't like cats?'

'She's the only girl I know of who's there . . .' His voice trails off. 'Project Manager. That's who she is. The Project Manager.'

'She said she lived there.'

'Um, yes. She lives there because she's — involved — with . . . my cousin.'

* * *

Marcus

I feel my cheeks heat up. What on earth made me say that? I mean, she is the Project Manager. But it's just weird for a project manager to live on-site, and I suddenly feel a bit stupid for allowing it. But if I tell Bea the truth, then she'll know I'm The Man, and that Carla works for me, and then she'll start to hate me . . .

My thought processes are making me cringe, and, let's be honest, not making me feel like I'm a decent human being.

I need to distance myself from Bea and her lilac hair and her green eyes and that scent of flowers and herbs that seems to be sticking to her, which is nothing to do with the little space we have found ourselves in.

For want of something to do, I reach out and rattle the gates again, making a few of those workman-like noises where you suck your teeth in and sort of go "hmmm, hmmmm, yes, this is going to cost you three times your budget, and I'll take cash in hand please . . ."

'A proper guvvy job,' I mutter.

'Guvvy what?'

'A guvvy job. Errrrmmmm — I think by that, I mean the . . . Project Manager won't need to know about this at the moment.' I look at Bea and something passes between us in a look. 'I can take a look while I'm here. See what I can find out from the other side. Bindweed, you say? And sticky jacks?'

A slow smile begins to twitch at the corners of her lips and her eyes glint mischievously. 'Yes. Bindweed. Do you know what it looks like? You'll know the sticky jacks. Everyone knows sticky jacks.'

I shake my head. 'Actually. No. I mean yes, I know what a sticky jack is, but not bindweed. What is bindweed? Please?'

'White, trumpety-sort of flowers. Roots can go down twenty feet. Massive vine sort of system. You'll see it.' She nods, as if that's all sorted now.

'Big job?'

'Very big job. But at least there'll be none of my frondy stuff hanging over to confuse you. The Man has put paid to that.' Her mouth purses up and the smile disappears.

'Okay. Right.' I smile a little weakly. I already feel that I've gone too far with the allusion to some fictitious cousin living there. I mean, it's an opportunity to get Bea onside, I guess — the more she hates The Man, and the more I seem to be helping her by hacking through the stuff on the other side of this gate, the more she's going to continue being nice to me. I had a glimpse of her when she was in her bee costume and she didn't look happy — and I've seen a little of how irate she can get today.

I know it's human nature to want to be liked and stuff, but I really, really do want to be liked by Bea.

I don't want to be banned from this amazing Garden — even though I've just discovered it today, it feels so welcoming and so friendly.

And if I didn't hear her incorrectly before, Bea has a pet bee. Called Bertie.

I've only known Bea for half an hour or so, but I already think she's incredible. She's clearly passionate about her Garden, and she's eccentric enough to be on the right side of crazy.

She's amazing.

So yes. The Man must remain a mystery, and I shall be the hero of the hour when I batter that door down for her. Well . . . batter the gates down.

But to be honest, I think I'd really love to find the key and avoid the battering bit. It would definitely make the access tidier and there'd be less mess to clear up afterwards . . .

And, of course, a tidy space would be a bit less noticeable to Carla as well.

* * *

Bea

So that's good. Marcus is going to do some weeding, and I've learned a little more about The Man — even though I don't like what I hear at all. Regardless, I'm very glad I've got Marcus Rainton on board.

'Okay, well, shall we head out of here?' I indicate the little dell we're currently standing in. 'Then you can enjoy the rest of the Garden and, with any luck, you'll put in a good word for me with The Man. Tell him he's unreasonable and my plants don't do it deliberately — well, maybe some of them do. Serotina's a little feisty when she wants to be —sorry, Serotina's the honeysuckle.' I nod across to her. She quivers with indignation, but she knows I'm right. 'That's what I call her. But you know, she was here long before he was.' Serotina quivers again and all the little flower heads nod enthusiastically.

Something flickers across Marcus' face but then he switches on a professional smile. He's obviously unused to people addressing plants like you might a friend, but I think it's a mark of mutual respect if you do that.

'Sure. Okay, I'll get back into the main garden and finish off having a walk around, then I'll pop back to the Visitors' Hut. Did I see a sign for annual passes there?'

'Yes, indeed you did.' I nod as enthusiastically as Serotina and switch on a professional smile to rival Marcus'. 'I'll be happy to sort one out for you. It works out; if you have three visits, you've made your money back.'

'Perfect.'

'Great. Thank you for discovering . . . this. I knew it had to be here somewhere. I can clear it on my side now, and you can ask your cousin to clear it on his side, or maybe even that woman can organise it — and then we'll have a thoroughfare.' I smile, but hey ho. Of course it doesn't matter if we have a thoroughfare or not, does it? I'm still technically banned from his side. But I suppose it'll look nicer and sort of intriguing, won't it? So the visitors can ooh and aaah about it, Maybe I can capitalise on the magical side of bees — bees in your garden indicate the blessings of the fae — or the Cousin Fae in my case — so it might be nice to add a bit of a fairy garden here . . .

My mind is racing ahead of me and I know I'm doing that thing where I look, to the outside world, as if all my neurons have stopped firing and I'm staring gormlessly into space. But really, I'm just thinking — "Thinking" with a capital T, that is.

'Umm — Bea?' Marcus' voice shakes me out of my plotting, and he taps me on the shoulder as I come back to full awareness. There's a little jolt as he touches me; not unlike a nettle sting but a lot more pleasant, and it sets all my nerves a-tingling. 'Bea? Are you okay?'

My eyes meet his and they lock for a moment. He looks a bit shocked too, but that's usually the reaction I get from a companion when they see me enter the Thinking zone, so I shake it off. I'm pretty sure he wouldn't have felt anything remotely jolty when he touched me.

'I'm fine, Marcus. I was just Thinking — Thinking of what I can do with this space when we're all tidied up. Ho hum. Okay — it's this way out, just follow me so nothing trips you up.' I know there are a few plants who might do that as a bit of a joke, but nobody ever finds it as funny as they do; Marcus should be safe if he comes with me.

'It's pretty . . . magical in here, isn't it?' His voice does seem full of awe as we duck and dip around the plants.

I smile ahead of me at nothing. 'Pretty magical is one way to describe it,' I say. And he seems to accept that.

Which is good.

Very good.

* * *

Marcus

I spend another hour or so wandering in Bea's Garden. Honestly, around every corner, just as you think you're coming to the end of it, there's something else to entrance you. It's beautiful and it's tranquil and yes — magical. Just as I told Bea earlier.

Finally, I think I've covered it all, and find myself heading back to the Visitors' Hut. I walk into the building, and am immediately enveloped in the delicious scent of herbs and flowers and all things summery. A quick glance around the little shop shows me a room with candles and balms and lotions and potions galore on the shelves, as well as a few jars of honey for sale.

'All made in the Garden. Maggie, who painted the sign — she and her sister, Isa, sometimes pop along to help me restock. Isa's fifteen or so, I think. Fifteen going on thirty.'

I jump as Bea's voice startles me. I turn and she's behind the desk, grinning. 'Sorry, I was just on my hands and knees under there, picking up yarn. Fae's got a terrible habit of shedding her yarn when she brings her crochet and knitting in — every so often I need to go on a purge.' She holds up a sheaf of brightly coloured wool. 'Waste not, want not. I'll leave it in a pile outside, and if the birds want it for their nests, they can have it.'

'Okay.' I can't help smiling back, and I want to keep the conversation going. 'Isa? Fifteen going on thirty, you say? But she's good at—' I wave my hand at the stuff on the shelves '—this sort of stuff?'

'Very good. Too good, really.' A thoughtful expression flits across Bea's face. 'That's why Nessa needs to sort her out.' I must look confused, as Bea laughs again. 'Nessa, Schubert's human, says Isa has "witchy propensities" and needs some training so she doesn't cause chaos. Says something about her not knowing her own powers yet.' Bea shrugs. 'Anyway, that's another story. Did you enjoy the Garden?'

I blink at the thought of Schubert the cat having a human, as opposed to having an owner, but I suppose it does make sense. 'Yes,' I say to Bea, when I've processed that thought. 'The Garden was great. There's just something about it that I can't quite put my finger on.'

'I think the Garden has its own "witchy propensities",' she replies. 'If you sit still in it long enough, it'll talk to you, I swear.'

'You mean the Nature Spirits will make themselves known?' Even as I say that, a weird shiver runs up my spine. I was doing some research a while ago, when Hidden Architecture explored the remains of a formal monastery garden in Yorkshire — and before I knew it, I was scrolling through some blogs

50

about the mystical and medicinal properties of plants. Someone mentioned Nature Spirits in one of those, and I glossed over it. But here, now, the words have just slipped out and I suddenly understand totally where that blogger was coming from.

'I mean exactly that.' Bea looks at me with an odd sort of respect. 'I'm glad you get it. It's just a shame The Man doesn't.' She purses her lips together and begins to look angry, so I quickly change the subject.

'Ummmm, I think I'd like to buy an annual pass,' I say.

'Oh!' Her face immediately clears and she smiles again, the dimples in her cheeks dipping in and out. 'We just need to fill a form in. Here we go.'

She produces a form, and then a pen, and I look at the details. Name, address, phone number, email . . . all the usual stuff. But hang on a minute — address. Address! I can't put Glentavish House down. But I can put my Islington address down. It's not a lie, I do own the place, so down it goes.

'Ooh. Islington,' says Bea when she reads the form and writes her own bits and bobs on it. 'That's exciting.'

'I like it,' I say, handing my money over to pay her. I do like it. It's a great base for work; I like Glentavish House too. Glentavish is supposed to be my bolt-hole, but it's pretty much Carla's playground at the minute — and that's not great, if I'm honest. I feel like I'm being unfair to Glentavish by not being here more often, and I guess it's not surprising that Carla is taking control of it in such a way . . . But Bea is chatting again, ringing my money through the till, and I turn my attention back to her.

'So I'll add your name to the mailing list, if you like, and you'll get our newsletter.' She shuts the drawer of the cash register firmly. 'Then if anything exciting is on when you're visiting the area, you'll know about it first. Because I suspect he,' she inclines her head in the direction of my house, 'won't tell you what's going on. He's not interested at all. There you go. One annual pass.'

She hands it over to me with a flourish. Tucking it into my wallet, I smile at her. 'Brilliant. Thanks. Okay — I'll head over to the house now and see if I can start looking for the key for that secret gateway. It's pretty exciting really, isn't it?'

'Very exciting.' She nods. 'I do hope you find it — I hope you find it before The Man stops you from looking, anyway. Let me know.'

'I'm sure that won't be an issue,' I reassure her.

'Thank you so much,' she says again. 'I do appreciate it. I really do.'

And she smiles again.

CHAPTER FIVE

Bea

Now he's a very nice man. Marcus Rainton. Who would have thought it? I mean, he always seems nice and smiley on television, but you never know, do you? Some of these famous types can be quite diva-ish, or so I've heard. I haven't met many, to be honest. In fact, have I ever met any famous types . . . ? I don't think I have.

Nessa knows quite a few famous people through her husband's work. Ewan is a screen writer for the movies, and Nessa always speaks very highly of the people she knows. I smile as I busy myself scooping the rest of Fae's discarded yarn into a pile. It's a different world. I'm happy here, with my plants and my Garden and my bees. A high-powered life doesn't appeal to me. And plants don't answer back.

Well, most of them don't. I have the odd feisty one who sometimes has to be tamed, and if you catch Agnes, Albertine and Callisto on a bad day, those girls can give you nasty scratches with their thorns. My pretty rose-girls can be an unholy trinity when they want to be.

'Islington,' I mutter again, looking at the address. It sounds very glamorous, but I'm sure that Glentavish House and my Garden can offer him a bit of respite from the world of television and socialising, so it's nice he's up here. And he's bought an annual pass, so hopefully he'll be back soon as well.

I add his name and email to my database, and, while I'm on the computer, I start typing out my newsletter. The Honey Festival is coming up in August, and although I've got those advertising leaflets sorted, it's always a good idea to let my annual pass holders know what's going on. Some of them live quite far away and might need a little bit more notice, after all.

Like Islington.

* * *

Marcus

I walk back to Glentavish House, and loiter a bit on the narrow lane that leads up to it from the Garden. I feel remarkably chilled and at peace, and yes — at one with Nature after spending some time in that environment.

Although I must confess that a gateway in the garden wall would be a much quicker and much more effective route for me to take. I wonder whether if we cleared the area and I did manage to find some sort of key — or even called a locksmith in to change the lock that's on there — I'd still have to report to the Visitors' Hut and show my annual pass to Bea before I wandered around the Garden? The thought makes me smile.

I'd quite like to work through all the outbuildings this weekend, I think, and see if I can find anything that looks like a key to the gates. Obviously, the locksmith is an option, but for some reason I really want to open that long-forgotten gateway with the key that belongs to it . . . if that's possible.

My daydreams are shattered, though, as a furious-looking Carla bears down on me as soon as I set foot in the house.

'Marcus! I've been looking for you all over! Yoga ended ages ago.' She looks angry and is waving something at me.

My heart sinks as it's probably an invoice or a blueprint or something. I actually don't want to be bothered with anything like that. I feel, at this moment, the most important thing is that the garden gets sorted and I get those gates open.

My priorities feel as if they have suddenly shifted, or at least become a little more garden-based than house-based. There's probably something deeply psychological about that. I want to open the gates to a calmer, more gentle world — a world that's inhabited by a girl with lilac hair and a bit of an attitude — and not stress over trying to change the heart of Glentavish House and drag it, ever so reluctantly, into the twenty-first century. But Carla's clearly demanding something and I close my eyes and take a breath before I respond, trying to hang on to the calm, meditative feeling I was just enjoying. I can't not listen to her; she's working on my house, after all.

'Did you enjoy your yoga then, Carla? Do you feel zen and calmed?'

'Of course I don't feel zen and calmed. I did feel zen and calmed, but not now. There's some sort of festival going on in that place next door soon. Did you know anything about it?' I open my mouth to respond in the negative, but Carla is already talking again and it's pointless trying to answer. 'It's going to impact on my project chart,' she says. 'I found this leaflet in the town — in the actual yoga studio, in the café area. Why didn't she tell us it was happening? You'd think as you're neighbours, you'd have a right to know when the lane is going to be clogged with traffic and people are going to be piling in. Strangers, random strangers, who might just want to get a little too close to the property. I am assuming you didn't know? Because you would have told me, wouldn't you?'

I sigh. 'I didn't know. But I honestly don't think that the type of visitor the Garden attracts will cause too much mayhem. What sort of festival is it, anyway?' I hold my hand out and she shoves the leaflet at me. 'Oh. A Honey Festival. So it's not even a festival-festival. Nothing like Glastonbury or Leeds or the Edinburgh Fringe.' I hand the leaflet back to her. 'It's a few hours of families coming to buy honey and honey-related products. And cakes and coffees as well, I suspect. Sounds quite nice.'

'But look at the date! Things move fast in this business. I mean, events happen quickly.'

'Why would I have an event on?' I look at Carla and frown. 'Why this obsession with having events on the property?'

She has the grace to blush. 'Well, you just don't know. Retreats. That sort of thing. You said you'd consider it. Or you might have been hosting your own garden party or something. Or had visitors coming to see the finished project. Family. Friends. Anyone.'

'Like I say, Bea's Honey Festival won't impact us in the slightest. Anyway.' I nod at the leaflet, my heart sinking a little. What a shame. 'I'm working that weekend — I'll be in Islington. So I wouldn't be hosting a knees up. And I think I'm a long way from having a retreat.' I mean it ironically, of course. A plan for a retreat is not in my near future. 'From what I can see, workmen are still coming and going in swarms. Look, why don't you take that weekend off to avoid it, if it's going to bother you that much? You could have a little break. You're knocking yourself out over this place, you're rarely away from Glentavish — and it's my house at the end of the day. It's not worth you getting stressed over. I'm paying you, and the last thing I want is my workforce going off on the sick. Do something nice to help yourself chill out that weekend. Hey, look — how about I relieve you of duties and call in some other people to assist in getting it done? Take the weight off your shoulders. It's a massive project, and, yes, it's good for your portfolio and for some exposure, but maybe it was too much to expect you to—'

'No!' Her refusal is shrill and scary. Her eyes are huge and glinting madly. I quail. 'I want to do it. It's experience. It's exposure. And it'll be done the way I want it, to my standards. Just let me get on with it. Don't call anyone else in — and don't get involved. I can handle it. I need to do this!'

'Okay!' I hold my hands up and shake my head. 'If you're sure. But at least let me take you out tonight as a thank you for what you've done so far. We can have a drink, have some food. Not listen to tarpaulins flapping in the breeze, and not worry about the state of the garden.'

'The garden,' sniffs Carla, 'is the least of my priorities. But yes. A drink might be nice.' There's a spark in her eye now. 'I can tell you all about my new yoga class. Bikram yoga — hot yoga. It's divine.'

I smile to myself. That sounds like my idea of hell, but it's really nice to see Carla excited about something that isn't ripping the heart of Glentavish House out — even if she means well by doing it.

CHAPTER SIX

Bea

It's a couple of weeks after Marcus visited and bought his annual pass. A couple of weeks closer to my lovely, lovely Honey Festival as well. Squee! I love the Festival, I really do. And it's also the day where Fae has invited me over for an evening of nibbles, wine and a DVD.

We do this every month or so. Fae knows how much I loathe my rented flat, and the fact it hasn't got a garden — so I think some of this is partly pity, and I do love sitting in her garden if I get the chance. She's created a Moonlight Garden, which is all white and ethereal and comes to life with the full moon. It's unutterably beautiful.

Our girly nights used to be just the two of us, but now it seems pretty fluid who'll be there. I don't mind either way. If it's just us, we have a good old girly giggle. More often than not, Tavey is there, and, bless her, she's a sweetie, although the cakes and bakes she brings along can some-times be rather random and taste like decade-old cobwebs and sawdust, depending on what ingredient she's decided to use. I can just about tolerate the beetroot cake, but Fae hates it — and although Tavey's lavender cupcakes are quite tasty, she always puts way too much lavender in. She soaks lavender in milk or something overnight, and adds that to the batter, then does something with lavender for the icing and then adds a sprig or two to the top of the cakes for decoration. We usually end up in a sleepy stupor if we have more than one of them.

Tonight, Alfie is here, so it's not truly a girly night — but oddly, we've also got the company of Isa and Schubert.

Schubert wraps himself around my ankles as I walk into Fae's untidy, ramshackle, but hugely welcoming cottage and greets me with a pleasant 'mow wow'.

'Good evening, Schubert,' I reply. 'To what do we owe this pleasure?' It is clearly the right thing to say to him, as he seems to grow in self-importance and pride and then adds an extra-warm 'mow wow'.

'We just thought we'd come and be sociable. Nachos?' Isa sticks her head out of the kitchen and waves a container shaped like a Mexican hat at me. I see cheese and salsa and sour cream and guacamole baked onto the side in big drips. I can never resist nachos, so I take a couple and crunch them as I walk into the room.

I wipe my hands on my shorts — I know, but they've had all sorts wiped on them and it's kind of just a habit now — and sit down on a footstool, moving a multi-coloured crochet blanket onto the floor. A large glass of something cold and alcoholic is pressed onto me by Fae and I accept it gratefully.

Isa follows me in and offers me more nachos as she takes up residence on a rocking chair. 'And anyway, I wanted to chat to you about the Honey Festival,' she says. 'So when Uncle Alfie said he was coming here, I asked Mum and Dad if I could come too, and they said yes — on condition I brought Schubert with me, for some reason.' She looks confused for a second, as though wondering why anybody would choose not to spend a Saturday night with Schubert. 'Anyway, Maggie cried and said she wanted to come but I said it was all about homework really and it wasn't very interesting. But, of course, it is interesting, because I'm getting involved.'

'Are you?' Alfie looks shocked. 'And rewind — Nessa dumped Schubert on your parents this weekend?'

'Yes, Uncle Alfie.' Isa looks at him like he's grown an extra head. 'Nessa's in London. You know this. And I'm involved because it's part of my IT course at school. I have to do a project and shit, and this is it. I'm helping market the Honey Festival!'

'Hmm,' Alfie says, staring at Schubert. 'And mind your language, Isabel.' Schubert has his bum in the air and he's using his claws to try and hook a nacho that's fallen off the dish and is currently under Isa's chair. 'I'd say I was glad I told Nessa I had plans this weekend when she rang me on Thursday,' continues Alfie, 'but I've ended up with Schubert anyway, haven't I?' Alfie's shoulders slump a little and he looks sort of defeated.

Tavey is sitting on a cushion on the floor, staring at the cat. A box of cupcakes is by her side and Schubert is very much ignoring the cakes and wanting that nacho. I hide a smile and wonder what the heck she's brought with her this time—

'Kale,' mutters Fae. 'Kale and lemon. I know. Exactly. Oh, he's a good boy. He's such a beautiful boy.' She coos at the cat and reaches down from her perch on the squashy sofa to pat Schubert's bum affectionately. Schubert does not move and his bum remains in the air. He's still focused on hook-a-nacho. His tail waves slowly as he apparently considers his next move.

I tear my attention away from the evidence that Schubert's hunting instincts are still there somewhere in that large, soft body of his and look at Fae. Well. We're all here, so we might as well cut to the chase and talk Honey Festival . . .

Yay!

'So later we talk Honey Festival. Right now, we talk Marcus Rainton.' Fae sideswipes me.

'Who?' I blink at her, startled.

'The Man.'

'What? Oh, he's not The Man,' I say confidently. 'The Man is his cousin.'

What is it with people thinking Marcus is The Man? Didn't Nessa think the same? Ridiculous thought!

'Really? He's not The Man?' That's Tavey. 'Oh — that's all right then. I say, I saw a picture of Marcus Rainton in the local newspaper a few days ago — he was out for a drink in the Distillers Arms, and he's with a woman in it.' She pauses for effect and looks around.

'Did someone poop him?' Isa adds with a snigger. 'Soz — Mags says that. Poop. Not pap. Like in paparazzi.' She grins around at us, and I see Alfie put his head in his hands and shake it despairingly. My talents don't lie in mind-reading, but at that moment I can truly sense it — and his mind is saying something like "Why me?"

'Yes, he was pooped. I mean papped.' Tavey blushes then giggles and I deduce she's already had a couple of Fae's famous gin cocktails — well, at least she's had enough to make her snigger at the word "pooped", maybe not quite enough to sample her own kale and lemon cupcakes.

'That's because they're disgusting.' I look quickly at Fae, then I realise Isa made the comment. I'm not even going to respond. Isa crunches on a nacho and stares at Tavey. 'Go on then,' she urges. 'What's the woman like?'

'Why do you even care?' asks Alfie in surprise.

'Because Mum thinks Marcus Rainton is pretty hot,' says Isa with a grin. 'She said Mags would have been a Marcus if she was a boy. So I want to know what sort of girlfriend he has.'

It's a fair point, I think. Also, I'm intrigued myself. I batter down a little note of disappointment at the fact he might have a girlfriend, but ho hum, let's not dwell on that one.

'It's not a very good picture.' Tavey frowns. 'I mean, this is the local newspaper, and I suspect it came from a smartphone.'

'No excuse,' mutters Ms Teen Social Media Guru. 'Can you tell at all what she looks like?'

'Just a "mystery woman".' Tavey shrugs. 'Long hair in a ponytail. Looks thin from the back.'

'I wonder if it's that horror who you chased with a mallet, Cousin Bea?' muses Fae.

'I didn't chase her!' I'm indignant. 'But she was awful. Gosh, I hope it wasn't her!' I realise I'm more bothered by that thought than I should be, really. What does it matter to me who Marcus Rainton spends his time with?

'Schubert tells me he's seen a project manager there,' says Isa. 'It might be her.'

Nobody queries this statement. Like everything to do with Schubert and the McCreadies, we just accept it.

'Ohhhh — the one in the hard hat?' interjects Fae. 'Near the flappy stuff.' She flaps her hands, demonstrating the tarpaulin, I presume.

Again, I don't question how Fae knows that.

'That's the one,' agrees Isa. 'Maybe she is the woman you chased, Bea.'

'Once again. I did not chase the woman! But she did look quite official,' I say. 'However, she wasn't wearing a hard hat.'

'Probably working in her office.' Isa nods as she crunches through more nachos.

'Mow wow.'

'Yep, you said you'd spotted her in there. Here you go. Good boy.' Isa chucks a very cheesy nacho towards Schubert. He thanks her politely (I think), and nibbles at it delicately.

'Wait, what? Schubert has seen her in her office?' Now I'm little confused. When did Schubert go over there to have a look at her office?

'Schubert enjoys constitutionals,' says Isa. She chomps on another nacho and glugs down half a glass of coke. 'Can I . . . ?' she asks, turning towards Fae and gesturing to a vodka bottle on the table.

'Absolutely not!' That's Alfie. 'Do you want your father to kill me? Do you want that, Isabel McCreadie?'

Isa rolls her eyes. 'If I was in France, I'd literally actually have bloody alcohol in my toddler sippy cup. With my dinner.'

'Still no.'

There's silent teenage hormonal rage simmering beneath the surface, and even Schubert is quiet on the matter, preferring instead to studiously lick cheese off his paws; so Isa slumps down in her seat and simmers hopelessly without an audience.

Isa's bad temper is amusing, but I need to find out more about this woman Marcus was seen with.

'Marcus told me that he was only visiting the Big House — it's his cousin's place. I assume his cousin is The Man. I'm not sure who that woman is, but I'm sure she can't be romantically involved with Marcus because she's supposed to be with The Man. She said they were partners. But yes, it makes sense that she's also the Project Manager, and I know Marcus was going to try and intervene and suggest that the garden should be sorted, and the gateway cleared between the estate and my Garden. I suspect he's trying to do it on the quiet, away from the house and away from The Man.'

'That's a possibility,' says Tavey thoughtfully. She stares off into the distance for a moment, drumming her fingers on the cake box. I'm a little concerned that she's picked the box up and am actually quite worried what her next move will be. 'It's up to these poopers what they choose to portray, isn't it?'

I bite my lip, trying not to laugh at her. She really is very sweet and I don't want to upset her.

Or make her remember she hasn't offered those strange cupcakes around yet.

'That's what good journalism is all about,' I say, confident that the Marcus Rainton I'd met would not be the sort of person to collude with another person about chopping the heart and soul out of a beautiful Garden. He was more likely asking her if she'd seen any keys that might be helpful, or maybe seeing if they could prioritise the clearance of the borders and the gates.

I mean, he hasn't got much to gain from that, if I look at it logically — but I'm not really a logical person and my best friend is a bee. So to me, a nice, slightly wild yet on-the-surface-tamed border framing a gorgeous old gateway is much higher on my priority list than renovating an old cow shed or whatever it is that's covered in tarpaulin.

I mean, how many people are going to get the benefit of the cow shed, compared to the number of people who are going to get the benefit of a nice, calming garden?

'Minimal,' mutters Fae. 'The answer is minimal numbers.'

I raise my glass to her and nod.

She nods back and I know that my cousin and I need no words in order to understand the situation.

'So shall we start finalising the festival then?' I ask. Part of me thinks we need to get this sorted before alcohol takes over and everyone starts to look as spaced as Tavey.

'I suppose we should.' Fae nods in agreement. 'Is the car parking going to be at the same place as usual? Have we still got the signs from last year?'

'Yes, they're in the shed.'

'Excellent. And what about refreshments?'

'Whisk and Waffle,' says Tavey, although she seems to have issues pronouncing the words, means as she's under the influence of the gin cocktails.

'True,' I say, 'but we've got the coffee van coming too. Look!' I pull up a picture on my phone of my friend Pippa's little coffee van. It's absolutely sweet as sweet can be. There's enough room for two people — one driver, one passenger — in the cabin, and the back opens up and voila, there's a coffee machine! It should tuck away nicely at the edge of the car park, which is an unofficial car park, but one that all my visitors are welcome to use.

Everyone oohs and aahs at the van as they remember how sweet it is, and we move onto timings of other traders turning up, social media advertising (Isa), and honey gathering and important things like that. Of course, the honey gathering is mine and Bertie's remit, and no matter who else in our group expresses an interest in it (Isa), it will definitely only be Bertie and myself dealing with that (not Isa).

At the end of the evening, we're all pleasantly swimmy with Fae's cocktails (except Isa), and Schubert is fast asleep on his back, legs wide apart, snoring his head off. I notice that he has Catnip, his favourite toy, with him this evening, and he's resting his furry cheek on the disgusting old thing quite contentedly.

Isa looks at him for a moment and smiles. 'He's still got some work to do, Bea. But don't worry. He'll get it sorted soon.'

'Right . . .' I say. I wonder if it's worth asking the obvious question at this point and clarifying exactly what Schubert still needs to do—

'No,' says Fae confidently. 'He's thinking about the best way to approach it.'

So I don't pursue the issue any more.

* * *

Marcus

Neither Carla or myself are happy about the fact someone took a photo of us in the Distillers Arms, or that it ended up in the local newspaper. I wasn't happy because, well, it's an invasion of privacy, isn't it? And I'm not a huge, mega-celebrity, so a) I'm unused to that sort of attention, and b) I wasn't under the impression that anyone would be remotely interested in me or who I was out with. Also c) is the fact that Bea might see that picture and pick up on the fact that it's Carla, who she clearly had that spat with, and realise that I'm more invested in Glentavish House than she thought I was. Also d) Bea might think Carla and I are together, and not just friends or colleagues, but I'm trying not to think about that too much.

It's a bit of a worry that Bea may think either of those things, and I know I only have myself to blame for point c (because we aren't acknowledging point d) — but it's that thing, isn't it? Where the longer a lie goes on, the more you realise there's a much bigger chance of getting caught, and the worse it will be when you do eventually get found out — because you inevitably will.

65

Carla doesn't like it because of a) there's only an a) reason for Carla — a) is that they got the back of her head and she wanted to be recognisable.

Oh well.

Anyway, there's nothing we can do about it, and hopefully those copies of the paper will be wrapping somebody's fish supper up by now, or lining a rabbit hutch or something. The more important thing for me to consider right at this moment is how to tackle the bindweed which is choking up the gate between Glentavish House and Bea's Garden.

Also, my ulterior motive is that if Bea does see that newspaper article, and puts two and two together, that she can realise I'm on her side really.

Or so I tell myself.

I look at Carla, who is scrolling through her phone at the breakfast table (it would be nice to have a bit of time to myself here, to be honest, but I can't just kick her out of the house and the room she's taken over — I'm only here for a few days after all) and reach over to tap her hand. 'Hey, Carla. Do you have any plans for today?'

'Hmm? What? Plans?' She looks blank for a second, then shakes her head. 'No. Although I'm going to see if I can get a guy out to look at the electrics in the studio, and—'

'Studio?' I ask. 'What do you mean by "studio"?' I'm confused.

· 'Oh! Did I say studio? Sorry.' She lifts her phone up and waves it around. 'I'm reading about the studio facilities in the town. They've just had some work done to attach some yoga swings to the ceiling so we can do aerial yoga. Very exciting. No — I meant the outbuilding with the tarpaulin. Could be a studio in the future though. Somewhere you can use as a commercial building, anyway. I'd run a session as a taster, and you would be safe in the knowledge that I had it all under control. You wouldn't have to lift a finger. In fact, you wouldn't need to be involved at all.'

'Sounds good to me.' Being involved in a session of anything yoga-related is nothing I want to do. At any point. 'Is the damp proof sorted then?'

'Almost. I just thought I'd get some quotes. You know, for going forwards.'

'Okay.' Part of me is still unsure as to the wisdom of doing so much to that old building, but there was a lot of scope for development in there, and if I don't go down the commercial route — or until I do decide to do that — the building will be a good space to keep things like the ride-on mower I want to get. I've always fancied a ride-on mower. I could whizz it around the big lawn and keep it neat and tidy. That's probably as far as my horticultural skills go, if I'm honest, but I digress. 'So do you have to do that today? Do you need to be here? Or do you want to do something else? Go somewhere? Take some time off the project? I'm happy for you to have a break, you know?'

'I really need to get cracking with it, I'm afraid.' She pouts at me, as if she's really sad that she can't go and do anything else. But I can tell by her eyes that she's quite excited to call guys about electrical quotes; there's a definite spark in her pupils that tells me so.

'Fine — I'll have a rummage in the old potting shed, then,' I decide. I smile at her. 'I won't leave you on your own to deal with guys. You can come and get me if you need me to—'

'Marcus!' her voice is almost a squawk. It's definitely indignant. 'Do you seriously think I need you to supervise me? I'm the Project Manager, for God's sake. I can handle workmen!'

'No! Of course not.' I'm a little taken aback. 'I just thought it would be nice if I was there. It's my property after all, and I want to be involved.'

I do, actually. I do want to be involved. It's beginning to seem, again, like the Glentavish House Restoration Project is being taken out of my hands, and that feels a bit odd — like I'm removed from the old place in a way I can't quite describe.

'Marcus. There is absolutely no way on earth I need you hanging around my office today,' says Carla firmly. 'I've told you before that this is my project and I'm going to see it through.'

'But it's my house,' I try. Even to me, it sounds whiny and pathetic and a bit "mine, mine, mine".

'My project though,' she fires back. 'We agreed that, so I could get my name out there. It could lead to all sorts of opportunities. I don't want it getting out that you had to handhold me like a baby all the way through it.'

I don't think that offering to give Carla support with some electrician visits is handholding, but clearly we have very different ideas about that.

'Fine,' I say, because I don't want to cause a fight over my breakfast. 'If you're happy to do that, I'm definitely going to rummage in that old potting shed and try to find some gardening equipment.'

Carla narrows her eyes, as if she's just registered the words "rummage" and "potting shed". And "gardening equipment".

'Why do you need gardening equipment?' she asks.

'Because I want to make a start clearing that border at the bottom.'

'Which border?'

'The one against the wall. Right at the bottom. The one with Bea's Garden on the other side.'

Carla rolls her eyes. 'Oh, I see. You're going to go down there and make a start clearing it. You who knows absolutely nothing about gardening or weeds or anything like that. You are going to make a start?'

'Yep.'

'Okay. Well. Have fun digging in the dirt!'

I know "fun" and "dirt" aren't two things that sit happily together in Carla-world.

'That's a bit unreasonable,' I say. 'You just told me you didn't need me up at the house. You concentrate on the house and let me deal with the garden.'

'You're doing it to appease that madwoman, aren't you? For the next time she decides to trespass on the land.'

68

'I honestly think her falling off that wall into the garden was a mistake. Good grief, Carla, why would she want to come and face your wrath voluntarily? The reason is simple. You've made it clear to me that it's way down the priorities list. I'm going to have a go at it myself, because you don't want me interfering with the main project. Which, apparently, you have in hand so it's no biggie.'

'Fine. Well. Enjoy it.' She stands up, pushing her chair back. 'And, truly, I don't need you hanging around the outbuilding anyway. I have it all under control. I know what the best way forward is, so I'll deal with it, okay? I don't need your face judging everything.' She grabs her iPad from the counter and taps on it as she turns to walk out of the room. She looks every inch the efficient Project Manager.

In the past, I've been told I've got a very expressive face. Basically, that's a polite way of saying my face says what I'm thinking, even if it's uncomplimentary. Yes, I'd be useless at poker. Which is why I'm still a bit baffled as to how Bea hasn't yet picked up on the fact that my cousin does not own Glentavish House, but I do.

'Okay.' I nod to her retreating back and doff an imaginary cap. 'I know my place, ma'am. And that be in the potting shed, ma'am.'

But she's already gone, so the sarcasm is lost in the ether. The effect of my Mellors-the-Gamekeeper impression is also lost.

Never mind. I can hear the tap-tap-tapping of her high heels disappearing along the wooden-panelled hall, so I stand up and head out of the back door, towards the potting shed.

It's more of a squelch-squelch-squelch for me, as it's rained overnight and the pathway to the shed is muddy. However, I suspect that the muddiness of the soil will actually make it easier to pull weeds out, so it doesn't bother me, and I've already booted up appropriately.

As I approach the shed, I see a big black shape sitting outside the door. I do a double take. It seems that the big black shape is largely big black fur and two piercing green eyes. There's quite a stern expression in those eyes, and I find myself stopping, as the big black furry shape is blocking my way into the potting shed, and for some reason I know it's not going to go anywhere fast.

'Mow wow,' says the shape. I realise it is Schubert, the cat I met in Bea's Garden, whose owner, as I seem to recall, has "witchy propensities". With the look the animal is giving me, I wouldn't like to assume that he doesn't know a thing or two about spells and witchcraft himself.

I shiver.

The cat continues to stare at me, his green eyes drilling into me, and for a mad moment I wonder: Does he know I own this place? And is he judging me for not telling Bea?

'Mow wow,' says Schubert, and I find the tone quite disturbing, if not a little judgemental.

We stare at one another for a moment or two, quite at an impasse, and then I shake my head and speak more confidently than I feel. 'I'm going to tell her. When the timing is right.'

'Mow wow.'

I get the sense he's saying, Really? You cowardly custard. You need to do it sooner rather than later!

I cringe inwardly and shake my head again. This is just my imagination, and yes, probably a wee bit of a guilty conscience. But it's nothing to do with this cat and this moment, so I brush the thoughts away.

'Anyway. I need to be in that potting shed,' I say.

The cat just stares at me.

'Out of my way. Go on. Shoo.'

The cat does not move.

'Schubert!' I approach him, intending to move him bodily out of the way if I have to.

'Grrrrrr.'

What the hell! I think the cat just growled at me.

Regardless, I try again, my hands outstretched.

'Grrrrr.'

Okay, that was a growl.

'Schubert!' I say. 'Please. Please would you shift out of the way?'

The cat glowers at me, but he seems to have responded to the word "please".

'Thank you,' I find myself saying. I move towards the door and try to open it, and he shuffles slightly along, so I'm sort of leaning over him and holding onto the doorhandle, rattling it in an increasingly angry fashion as I can't get it to open.

'Mow wow wow . . .'

I look down at Schubert. That sounded exactly as if he was laughing at me. 'It's not funny!' I tell him. 'You might be amused at this, but I'm not.'

'Mow wow.' He blinks at me, and it's almost as if he's saying, you fool of a man, of course it's funny.

'The main reason I'm trying to do this, Schubert,' I mutter between clenched teeth, 'is because I want to help Bea. I want to try and get rid of some of that bindweed, or whatever it is, and clear the gates for her. And to do that, I really need to be in this damn potting shed! Because that is where all the tools are.'

'Mow wow?'

This time, he looks up at me, and he phrases his strange meowing as if it's a question. I pause and look down at him. I sense there's a bit of a battle of wills going on here.

'Yes. It's for Bea. To help her.'

'Mow wow!' There's a softening to the evil glint in his eye, and he leans heavily against the door. I've still got hold of the handle, and I wiggle it at the same time.

The door swings smoothly open and I almost fall into the musty old place.

'Hey! I'm in! Umm . . . thanks Schubert?' I'm not sure how much influence he had on that door opening, but it seems rather odd and coincidental that he's leaned against it and it's opened . . . perhaps it just needed a bit more weight—

'Mow wow!'

Okay, maybe not.

71

Anyway, I manage to step over Schubert and enter the potting shed. Or at least I think I've stepped over Schubert and managed to enter the potting shed, but he's suddenly in front of me and actually sitting on a table, licking his paws and staring at me again.

I blink. Then I check the area around my feet, and the area just outside the door, but there's no sign of him.

'Mow wow,' says the cat on the table, and it is definitely Schubert. For a cat of that stature, he can move fairly quickly, I have to say.

'Okay. Well. Enjoy the view,' I tell him. 'I need to find some tools and then at least I can start to clear the area around that gateway, even if we can't open it.' I walk to the wall and look at the tools hanging there. They came with the house and, to be honest, like most things at Glentavish, I've never given them much thought. The agent said the sheds were "fully equipped for all gardening needs", but — as evidenced by my struggle with the door — to my shame, I've never been in the potting shed.

Carla spotted the potting shed when she first visited the place and went into ecstasies, as she thought it would be, and I quote, "a very bijou place for a hot tub". I said I thought otherwise, because where would I keep all the tools the agent had told me were in there? And she suggested that I could simply build a new shed and restock the equipment.

I didn't agree at the time, and I don't agree now, but thankfully the Project hasn't worked its way down to the potting shed yet — and neither has the Project Manager.

But back to the tools in the shed. Many of them look, to me, like instruments of torture — as I say, I'm no gardener — but I recognise a trowel and a pair of secateurs hanging up, and spot a hand-held fork alongside. They'll have to do.

I unhook them from the wall — they look a little rusty but serviceable enough — and I search for a wheelbarrow, as I have a feeling a bucket won't be enough to contain all the weeds.

'There we go,' I say with a grin, spotting a wheelbarrow and, bonus, some new gardening gloves still in their packet.

I toss the tools inside the barrow, open up the gloves and try them on for size. All good. 'Great. Schubert, I'm all set,' I say.

'Mow wow,' he acknowledges. The he lies down on his back with his legs stuck in the air and immediately begins to snore.

I shake my head and exit the potting shed, leaving Schubert to catnap while I go and tackle the weeds in the border.

CHAPTER SEVEN

Bea

Little Mags has offered to draw some pictures to help advertise the Honey Festival. Her only demand is that she is allowed to put Schubert in them.

I smile to myself as I remember Fae telling me this. Mags came along a couple of days ago and showed me how good her drawing skills are by creating a picture on the old chalkboard I have stashed in the Visitors' Hut. It was pretty good for a small child; a chalk drawing of a cat and a bee, sitting either side of a honey pot (a "hunny pott"). Isa took some arty pictures of it, and those shots are now zooming around the social media ether. Isa reckons she'll get extra credit for her course at school by doing it, so I don't think her actions are entirely selfless, or motivated by making her little sister feel important in any way, shape or form.

Anyway, it's all good publicity, and I'm taking advantage of the fact it rained last night and still looks a bit overcast this morning, to tidy up some of the flower borders in the Garden. I tend to find that people come later in the day when the weather is like this — almost like they're giving it time to clear up. But I've left the Honesty Box out at the Visitors'

Hut, so I just have to trust that any visitors I do miss will be — well — honest.

What they don't realise is that there is a certain magic to the Garden just after a rain shower — that amazing, earthy smell of petrichor just can't be beaten. Alfie is a scientist and tried to explain the mechanism behind it all to me once. I zoned out after the first mention of something like "it's the bacteria in the soil getting trapped in aerosols which are released when rain hits the soil, and the bacteria responsible for those aerosols are part of the Actinomycetales order of bacteria . . ." and hid a smile when Fae folded her arms, glared at him and said, 'Our noses are designed to like it, Alfie, because our ancestors relied on rain for survival.'

Whatever the explanation, I love the smell of it, and the little raindrops that gather on the petals and leaves are like tiny diamonds glinting in the sunshine, and it's all just beautiful.

So it comes as something of a surprise when I hear a noise on the other side of the wall. I'm at the part of the wall where Marcus discovered the gates; I chose this part of the border to work on because I've decided it'll be lovely to have the gateway exposed there like something out of The Secret Garden for the festival. Eventually, I think I might be able to make a bit of a feature out of it. It will have a certain Gothic glamour, I think, all rusted and partially hidden away by my flowers.

It would, of course, be much better to be able to open the thing, but that's a daydream and would serve no practical purpose whatsoever at the moment. I'm not allowed in The Man's garden (and nor would I want to be in it if Banshee Carla is on the prowl), and I certainly don't want The Man or his legion of the damned (Banshee Carla) in my Garden. So a Gothic Fantasy it shall become.

I've been there a little while, working hard, clearing bindweed and foliage away, pulling ivy gently from the wall and exposing more of the wrought iron work, and I'm quite happy; then I hear a strange noise from the other side of the gateway.

It's not possible to see who or what is creating the noise, because all I can see through the bits of ironwork I have exposed is a dense, green, leafy forest. There's a lot of weeding and clearing needed on that side. Part of me is itching to go in there and sort it out, but another part of me knows it's just more practical to concentrate on this side.

The noise I can hear is like a grunting, huffing animal noise. I vaguely wonder whether bears are still around in this area. Or wolves, maybe? Then there's a series of swear words, so I realise that it's a human beast hidden behind that thicket of bindweed.

More to the point, I can recognise the voice of the human beast. It's a voice that I'd expect to hear more in the environs of, oh, I don't know, Islington perhaps. Well, let's be honest, it's a voice I've heard a lot of recently, as I've been doing a lot of searching online for episodes of Hidden Architecture. One of the streaming services has all of the series available to download, so I've been enjoying a bit of binge-watching. I now know my corbels from my modillions, and will never buy a house with an oubliette.

I just felt as if I needed to understand a bit more about Marcus Rainton. I mean, I don't stalk all my annual pass holders — but when you have a sort of famous one, it's interesting. Especially as he managed to locate the gates.

And especially as he's pretty easy on the eye.

I look to the side and see a ladder propped up against the wall. I'm fairly sure I didn't leave a ladder there, but odd things happen in this Garden, so I don't quibble, but instead walk over to it and climb it.

Soon, my head pops over the wall and I peer down into the other garden, my arms folded on the top of the brickwork.

An interesting sight catches my attention. It's definitely Marcus, and he's dressed in a white T-shirt, a button-up grey shirt flapping open on top of it and those long cargo shorts they call "city shorts". He's also wearing a pair of muddy boots. I study his white T-shirt, and know from experience that it won't remain white for long if he's digging around in the garden.

I'm not studying it because of the fact it clings to his body in all the right places — oh no.

I watch him for a few minutes, finally deciding to shout down and tell him I'm here, because the speed of his weeding is actually quite painful to watch.

'Marcus!' I call.

He swears again and jumps, seemingly looking around for where my voice is coming from.

'Up here!' I say, and wave at him as he looks up. He grins at me and shades his eyes with his hand. However, it's the hand he's holding the trowel in, and he ends up with mud in his hair, so he swears again and tries to brush it out. It's now sprinkling his shoulders like confetti and yes, there we go, he's just got a big glob of the stuff on the white T-shirt.

'It's better if you let it dry,' I offer. 'Then it comes out easier. All you're doing is just mushing it around.'

'Thanks for the advice. That's what I get for trying to be helpful, is it?'

'Yes. I suppose that's unkind of me when you're trying to clear the garden and The Man obviously has no interest.'

'Oh, The Man,' says Marcus. 'It's funny you should say that, because—'

'Stop!' I say, closing my eyes and raising my hand. I saw that peculiar look in his eye when he began that sentence, and I realise he's uncomfortable with the subject. And I don't want to spoil our chat. 'It doesn't matter. Anyway, it's good to see you.'

'It's good to see you too, Bea. Yes, I'm here for a flying visit.'

'A nice place to visit. Better than a hotel.' If you can tolerate being around The Man, that is, I want to say — and I'm not sure that I, personally, could tolerate being around The Man for any length of time, but I'm not Marcus and he's maybe not as sensitive as me to The Man's attitude. 'But I have to say that you're making quite a mess of that weeding.'

There's a beat and Marcus folds his arms over his chest — more mud smears on the T-shirt. I could have told him so.

'If you're so good at it,' he says, 'why don't you pop over and help?'

77

'Well, you know I'd love to.' It's not a lie; I would. 'But I think I'm persona non grata with that project manager, sooooo . . .' I shrug. 'And anyway, there's the small issue of getting over there in the first place.' I reach across and tap the gates. 'If we had a key for this, it would be so much easier.'

'Ah. The Project Manager,' he says, 'and The Man.' And we're both silent for another beat. Then the silence is interrupted by a beep from a mobile phone.

* * *

Marcus

I look down at the pocket of my shorts in some surprise. I'd almost forgotten I had the phone with me. Another interruption, another instance of me being prevented from saying anything about this fictitious Man. ("I'm here for a flying visit". Really, Rainton?) The longer it goes on, the harder it's proving to find the right moment to confess. I should just come out and say it, but the very thought makes me go hot and cold all over.

'That's my phone then, I guess,' I say, and dig into my pocket to find the device. When I pull it out and read the text message, I feel a strange mix of emotions. It's from Carla:

> *Going to pop to yoga. Electrician can't make it today and new aerial class on in half an hour. I can make it if I hurry, so quicker to text you than come and look for you to tell you. See you later, C x*

'Okay.' I'm saying it more to myself than for anyone else to hear. Carla has gone out. She'll be gone for at least three hours, going by typical yoga-trip experiences — which means . . . 'You're safe. Carla has gone out. She'll be away ages, so you can come over and help. And anyway, even if she wasn't happy, she hasn't exactly got the biggest say in the matter.'

'Maybe not. But you haven't either, and I don't like her so I wouldn't want to come over if she was lurking around

78

anyway. Okay — how do I get in? I wonder if I can some-how haul the ladder over after me and clamber down . . .' Bea starts looking around, seemingly judging whether that's practical or not.

'I've got a better idea,' I hear myself saying. 'Sit on the wall and let your legs dangle — then you can sort of slither off and I'll catch you.' Then I feel my cheeks heat up. That's just a bit inappropriate, isn't it?

Then Bea surprises me by saying: 'Actually, that's not a bad idea. Let me just get a couple of things first, and I'll be back.' She disappears downwards again, her head dipping out of view, then there's a bit of a rhythmic thudding noise, as if she's chucking tools into a container of some kind, then she pops up over the top of the wall again, her cheeks flushed. 'Here. Just need a few tools. Can't abide working with any-one else's.'

She's hauling her trug over the top of the wall, then indicates that I should catch it as she lowers it gently down. I do so, and, when the trug is down, she shimmies around so her long, tanned legs are dangling over the edge. 'Watch out. Here I come.' She grins and slithers down, just as I suggested.

Somehow, I realise I've already got my arms open, and within moments, I've caught her around the waist and we've managed to get her on her feet on my side of the garden.

Suddenly, it feels a bit intimate and weird, with us both staring at one another, until she clears her throat and nods to the trug. 'Okay — you can let go now. I need to get to my tools.'

Horrified, I realise I'm still holding her, so I quickly unhand her and take a step backwards. I run my fingers through my hair, smiling awkwardly. 'Great — all sorted then. Show me how a Master Gardener would tackle this lot, and we'll go from there.'

'My pleasure,' she says.

And so we begin.

With Bea's instructions and demonstrations, ("No you're doing it all wrong, dig it out if you can, like this

— don't just cut it down, there are roots!" "Use a fork. Get the whole lot out. Every bit you leave in the ground will grow again!" "No, you absolutely cannot put that stuff in the compost heap — do you want to replant the thing? And spread it all over your garden in the process?") we manage to settle down into a routine. We both dig out as much bind-weed, ivy and sticky jack as we can and pile it all into the wheelbarrow. Then we take turns dumping the stuff into a separate pile at the far end of the path. I'm quite tempted to have a bonfire with it, but Bea says we can also put it in bags and get it taken away.

Listen to me; "we" can put it in bags. "We" can get it taken away.

There is no "we".

Not in the sense I'm making it sound like, anyway.

'We're doing really well with our pile!' says Bea eventually. We. Again. I push the thought of "we" or "us" out of my mind and switch on a smile to face her with.

'Yep. We are.'

We.

'Look — the gateway's cleared now, don't you think? There's still a bit of work to do on either side, but this is the most important chunk of it done. Amazing.' She's beaming at the newly exposed gates, and I can see straight through the intricate, rusty linework into Bea's Garden. It's astonishing.

'Wow.' I pause for a moment and step closer to the gate-way. 'It is amazing. Look — can you see how the designer created a pathway for your eye? A line from the main window of the house up there, through to the walled garden there — there would have been a focal point along it. They used to love putting things like sundials or fountains in for that.'

Bea comes closer to me, and I'm horribly conscious of her warm body next to mine, our arms almost touching, as we both peer through to the newly opened vista. 'I think the focal point was a folly,' says Bea, surprising me.

I look down at her. 'Really? Aren't I supposed to be the one who knows all about hidden architecture and what's

80

meant to be where? Yet you're the one who knows about this alleged folly?' I'm teasing her and she laughs as she looks up at me. She knows I'm teasing, which is good. 'Go on, then, clever clogs — tell me more.' I know the answer, of course, as I know what Lady Clementine dreamed of — but I want her to tell me. It seems important, somehow, that Bea should talk about it.

'I saw something in a local history booklet about it,' she says. 'I did lots of research when I came here, because one of my plans was to get it back to how it was. It turned out the Garden had other ideas though, and I ended up just going with the flow. There was an extract from someone's letter — a Lady Clementine Eliza Grey — who lived here when it was first built. She also talked about this gateway between the formal gardens and the estate. And it's always intrigued me.'

'Oh yes! Lady Clemmie. I know about her.' I'm sure she wasn't really called Clemmie, but Clementine Eliza is quite a mouthful. 'There's a portrait of her in the house.' I stop myself from suggesting Bea should come and have a look at it, because that's inappropriate and could open a whole new can of worms. 'She's quite pretty — she hangs in the salon on one side of the fireplace, and her husband is on the other side of it. Actually, she doesn't so much hang there; she's actually built into the wall — the portraits were painted onto it and a moulded frame, built into the plaster, put around them.'

'I guess that's a good way of ensuring your portrait won't get tossed away and you still get remembered years later,' says Bea. 'I wonder if it's based on the sketch in the local history booklet I read?'

'I know the booklet you mean, and I think it is.'

Bea smiles delightedly. 'How lovely! In the letter, if you remember, she says she's going to commission a folly — a Temple to the Four Winds, which is going to, and I quote, "reside in the centre of the walled garden, so one can gaze upon it from the House, and imagine oneself sitting in it, daydreaming, at the centre of the world."' Yes! That's exactly my understanding! 'I thought it was a lovely sentiment,' continues Bea, her eyes shining. 'I suppose her world might have been quite small and contained in those days, so at least she had somewhere she could daydream. I always wanted to find out more about her, but the Garden took over my time, and I didn't manage any more research. It's a shame.' She pulls a face. 'I do hope she had a long and happy life.'

'Hmmm.' I don't really want to tell her that Lady Clemmie died when she was twenty-four in childbirth. Instead, I settle for: 'I believe she was what they called "delicate" — three kids in three years was a lot for someone of her constitution, so she probably liked the idea of somewhere to escape.'

Bea is silent. Then: 'Oh. Okay. She died young then. Champion.' She pulls a face and I feel really bad.

'I'm sure the time she had on earth was happy,' I say pathetically. 'All the records I've seen suggest she was very happy in her marriage and loved Glentavish House. She looks cheerful in her portrait and her husband, Lord Archie Grey, is a handsome chap. I think you're right — her folly was going to be her Temple. Right there.' I point to the empty space through the wrought iron.

'I doubt she ever got her Temple, though. I haven't found any trace of it myself, that's for sure. It's such a shame. Can't you do some digging and find out if it ever existed? If there are any designs anywhere? Like you say, you're the expert on hidden architecture, after all.' Bea turns to me, and there's a little spark of hope in her eyes. 'I'd love to replicate it and put it where Clemmie wanted it. Now we can see through the gates again.'

I nod. 'Yes. I'll see what I can do.'

I feel Bea stiffen next to me. 'If The Man lets you rummage in his archives, of course.'

'I'm sure he will. Bea, I—'

'Oh heck!' Bea turns and looks up. It takes me a moment to realise that there's a bumble bee buzzing around her head. 'What is it, Bertie?' she asks. The bee buzzes frantically around her ear and her expression changes. 'Schubert. I see. Okay. We'll go and sort him out.'

The bee buzzes away, and if I could draw his flight path in the air, it would be a series of loop-the-loops.

'Schubert is apparently in the potting shed,' she says. 'Which is curious for two reasons. One, I didn't know he was around today. And two, how did he get here anyway?'

'I did see him in there earlier,' I admit. 'I didn't give it a thought. I thought you were looking after him.'

'Nope. Not today.'

She shakes her head and I want to ask whether she's concerned that Schubert is here. But she doesn't seem concerned; in fact, quite accepting of the situation. 'Anyway, he's fallen off the table and managed to get himself wedged.' She rolls her eyes heavenwards. 'So I'd best go and rescue him. Where is the potting shed, please?'

'Up this way.' I point, and she tosses her tools into her trug and wipes her hands down her shorts.

'Okay, thanks. You'd best come too. Then if the Project Manager sees me, you can stick up for me.'

I'd almost forgotten about Carla. There's been no message from her to say she's coming back, and then, just on cue, my phone beeps again.

My stomach somersaults as I pull it out of my pocket and read the message. Then I exhale in relief.

Going for drinks with friends. Taking your advice for some time out and won't be back until 5pm at earliest. C x

It's so very, very wrong of me, but I'm happy to read that message. So very happy. I don't want any drama, thank you very much, and I've known Carla a long time, so I know what she's like when she decides something, and I think she's decided she doesn't like Bea.

I grin at Bea. 'You're safe. She's caught up with some other project, so she won't be back until five. Let's go and rescue Schubert.'

'Great. Thank you.'

She doesn't ask why the Project Manager has texted me about her plans. Maybe she thinks my fictitious cousin texted instead . . .

I decide not to go there.

Instead, we start walking up the garden, chatting about the neglect that's quite evident around the grounds. I feel a bit embarrassed about it, and if I'm honest, it doesn't make me want to admit that I own the place. The fact of that matter is that I'm responsible for the neglect.

'I can understand that some parts of the house need renovating urgently,' says Bea. 'So a person has a usable bathroom, a bedroom, a kitchen and a lounge — but once that's done, I'd be moving onto the garden before winter sets in. I mean, winter is a good time to clear it out, but you really need to have a good look at the place in the summer so you can get an idea of planting schemes and what goes where . . .'

She makes a lot of sense, I think. I wish that Carla had been less enthusiastic about outbuildings and more enthusiastic about the garden now — it makes me want to cringe. Why on earth did I let her renovation plan get so far along the line without offering more suggestions and taking more of an interest?

I know I've been busy with work, and most of the time I just gave in for an easy time of it. In my mind, Carla and I had the same vision. In reality, Carla's vision has outscoped mine, and I think we've lost some boundaries along the way.

It's taken just a few hours with lilac-haired, green-eyed Bea to make a few things clear.

I need to have a think about what I can do — it's not a great situation to be in, is it? Carla thinks she owns the place, and Bea thinks A Man owns the place — and I'm the one who really owns the place. Awkward.

'Is this the potting shed?' We've reached the place, and I nod.

'Yep. The door was a bit sticky before but . . . oh. Oh, it's fine now. Great.' It's opened with no effort at all, and I realise I'm leaning over the top of Bea, and she's sort of tucked in the crook of my arm while I lean. Neither of us seems to think this is an issue, as neither of us makes any attempt to move.

'Great,' echoes Bea.

The door swings open, and I look at the table where I last saw Schubert — flat on his back, legs akimbo, snoring his head off.

And he's not there.

We stare in silence, both looking around the place. My eyes are adjusting to the gloom, because it's quite sunny out there now, and it's showing the potting shed up for what it is — a manky old wooden building full of spiderwebs and dead leaves.

'Oh my God!' breathes Bea. 'It's amazing in here! It's beautiful! Wow — The Man is so lucky! Look at these tools — just look at them!' She moves forward and brushes her fingertips over some of the instruments of torture I spotted before. But she seems to like them. 'Gosh — I'd love to come back in here and have a good old poke around.' She peers into the deepest recesses of the shed, and there is a huge smile on her face. 'But not now. Now, we have to find Schubert. I can't see him anywhere, can you?'

'He was on this table before.' I walk over to the table and see a round mark on the dusty surface, almost like a giant pom-pom was placed there and wiped around slightly to clear the spot. I follow some more marks in the dust, and can work out that he's slithered over the top somehow, scrabbled for purchase (I assume) then dropped over the side. Now I notice there are two black paws in the air, a tail and a rump.

Bea comes over and she must notice the marks too. 'I think he's wedged between the table and the wall,' she says.

'Mow wow.' Schubert sounds cross and dazed and muffled. 'Mow wow.'

Bea peers over the back of the table. 'Bless him. Come on, Mister. Up you come.' She reaches over, and looks as if she's going to grab his back legs and pull him up. Then she clearly thinks better of it. 'No, that's not going to work. I think we'll have to move the table. He's nose down in there, poor little sausage.'

It's the first time I've heard a Beast of that magnitude referred to as a "poor little sausage", but sausage is as sausage does, and I don't argue.

'Okay,' I say. 'I'll take this side of the table, and you take that one.'

We ease the huge oak table, which I don't think has moved for at least a century, away from the wall with a great deal of creaking and scraping, and finally Schubert elegantly slides down the wall into a giant black furball. He lies there for a moment before he wriggles around and his face appears out of the black mass.

'Mow wow,' he says, and stretches out. Then he turns around and licks something on the ground — which would have seemed quite vile, until I see what it is.

Bea notices what it is at exactly the same time.

'A key!' we both say together.

Bea looks at me and I look at her, and, wordlessly, she bends down to pick it up, then hands it to me.

'Shall we?' she whispers. 'Shall we?'

CHAPTER EIGHT

Bea

'Mow wow!'

Schubert's voice makes me jump and I look at him, then bend down to give him a big fuss, remembering my manners amidst all the excitement.

'Thank you,' I tell him. 'You are such a good boy! Such a good boy. Remind me to give you some tuna later.'

'But how do we know it's the key?' asks Marcus, staring at it. 'It could be any old key.'

'It could be,' I say, 'but it's not. Believe me. If Schubert has found it, and alerted us to it, then it's the very key we're looking for. Trust me. Trust him.'

'Mow wow.'

'Yes. Thank you. Schubert, are you supposed to be with anyone today? Does Nessa know where you are?'

Then my phone beeps. I take it out of my pocket and read the message.

It's from Isa.

Hey Bea. Schubert wanted to come and see you. Something about finding a key? I let him off the bus at your stop this

morning, so he'll have found what he wanted by now. Just tell
him to head back to the bus stop and we'll collect him. Unless
you want to hang onto him for a bit? Something about tuna?
If so, I'll get Dad to come over for him. Let me know xx

I read the message again and look at Schubert.

Schubert looks up at me and licks his lips.

I text Isa back: *Yeah, he's here. Promised him tuna. Will let*
you know when he's ready so your dad can get him. See you later xx

Then I relay the situation and the text conversation to
Marcus who, I have to say, looks confused. 'You'll get used
to his quirks,' I hear myself telling him. 'Just go with the flow
and you'll be fine.'

'But how did she know—how did he get here from the
bus stop?' He looks like his head is going to pop as he processes it. I reach out and touch his arm, meaning only for it
to be a reassuring pat, but there's that zing again and I jump.

Deliberately, I drop my hand and step back. 'Honestly.
Don't question it. Come on. Let's try this key and see what
happens. Schubert, do you want to come with us? You can
try the little cat-flap. Oh look! Here's Bertie come to say
hello to you!'

It's true — Bertie has zoomed over to us. He gives a little
buzz buzz of delight and darts in closer to his feline friend.

'Mow wow!' It's as excited as I've seen Schubert get in a
while and I smile at him — mainly so I don't have to meet
Marcus' eyes. Marcus looks a little freaked out, and I can't
say that I blame him. He grabs an old tin of oil in case the
lock is a bit - well — locky — and off we go.

Schubert gambols and frolics his way out of the potting
shed, which is certainly a sight to behold, especially as Bertie
is keeping pace. Together, the four of us walk back down to
the wrought iron gates, and I can feel my heart racing and the
excitement building with every step I take. Which is just a bit
mad, as it's only an old gateway at the end of the day, and we
haven't lost anything if the key doesn't open it.

But I'm absolutely certain it will.

We reach the gates and stand in front of them. I can tell Marcus feels the same as me. He weighs the key in his hands and I even detect a slight tremble to them. 'Do you think you can manage to get it in the lock?' I whisper. Whispering seems appropriate in such a charged situation — it almost seems as if we're about to perform some sacred ritual.

'I . . . think I'd like some help?' He whispers back, and our eyes meet. He holds out the key and I exhale, and somehow we are both grasping it and moving it closer to the lock . . .

'Mow wow!' yells Schubert in excitement, clearly energised and ready to rumble. 'Mow wow!' Then, I can only explain his action as a sort of shoulder barge as he runs towards the cat-gate at an angle.

'Schubert! Be careful!' I shout, leaving hold of the key in case I have to do feline first-aid, but it's too late — he's charged his way through the miniature entrance and has burst through into my Garden with seemingly no ill-effects. I am utterly stunned. There wasn't a creak, a groan or any resistance whatsoever to the gate — and he's the first one to have managed to break through that barrier.

'Mow wow, mow wow!' He's prancing around in the flowerbeds, clearly delighted with himself. Bertie is dive-bombing him and turning somersaults — too discreet to let Schubert know that he can come and go as he pleases due to the fact he can fly over the wall a lot more elegantly than Schubert can shoulder-barge.

Marcus blinks and turns to me. 'I'm just thinking — he met me at the potting shed earlier, but how did he even get over the wall? Or did he use that cat-gate? What did he do?'

I shake my head and say nothing, thinking of the random ladders I saw earlier. 'He's Schubert. Like I said: don't question it. Come on. Let's give this a go. We're too big for the cat-gate.'

'Of course. Yes. Right — here we go. Will I need the oil?'

'No. I don't think so. Let's just . . . see, shall we?'

Once again, he holds the key out and we grasp it together.

89

We line everything up and I find myself holding my breath as we ease the key into the lock and turn it . . .

There's a little bit of a moment where it seems as if it doesn't want to turn — but then there's a clunk and the double gate starts to open a little in the centre. I push at one side, and Marcus pushes at the other — and there's a creak and a groan and then they swing open.

'That's it! We're through!' I yell. I can't help but do a little happy dance — well, a big happy dance, and I look up at Marcus in delight.

His eyes are shining and there's a huge grin on his face. 'Come on,' he says. 'We do this together!' And he grabs my hand, and we run through the gates, laughing as we stumble and squelch through the still damp earth and end up on my side of the wall. He pulls me towards him, and suddenly — don't ask me how — I'm tilting my face up to his, and he's leaning his face down to mine, and then we close the distance and we should be in the middle of the most unexpected, the most spontaneous and the most magical kiss I have ever experienced . . . but instead we halt before our lips actually connect and our eyes lock and I just see confusion in his gaze — and we freeze.

Then: 'Bea!' A teenage squawk echoes through the Garden. And not just any teenage squawk. It's an Isabel McCreadie teenage squawk. Followed by: 'Shoooooobert. Buuuuuuuuurteeeee!' in a definite Maggie May McCreadie holler.

Marcus and I spring apart and stare at one another. 'Well now. That was unexpected,' I say. 'Not my usual pattern of behaviour, that. Almost kissing annual pass holders, I mean.'

'Mine neither. I'm so sorry. That was a complete mistake. I should never have . . .' His voice trails away. 'No, what I mean is—'

'It's a mistake, is all. It was excitement about the gate opening. Not to worry.' I paste a smile on my face and consciously move back another step or two. I'm trying hard not to hang onto that word "mistake" or put myself in the category of "mistake". Not the almost-kiss. Me. I was the mistake. What would a celebrity like Marcus Rainton want with kissing a gardener like me? I mean, I'm single, and part of me was hoping he was too . . . but maybe he's not. Or maybe he's just not interested.

Which makes me feel quite embarrassed.

Oh dear.

It's odd, isn't it, how you cling onto the most negative thing and don't celebrate the good stuff? Like that one-star Trip Advisor review the Garden got, because it didn't have a fancy-schmancy restaurant or soft play area. Not the tons of lovely four- and five-star reviews that praise the Garden. It's the one-star that I focused on for a whole month. And today, in this moment, I feel like a one-star review has been posted against me in a personal capacity.

Mistake.

Ho hum.

Oh well, just as well I'm not romantically interested in Marcus Rainton, isn't it? I tell myself. But I never was a good liar, even to myself, and I feel my cheeks heat up as I think that, actually, we've had a lovely time this morning; and on the few times we've met each other, I've definitely been attracted to him.

Argh.

Anyway. It's obviously not reciprocated, so time to sweep those feelings away and try to concentrate on the moment. Which is filled with even more bellowing from the McCreadie girls as I hear them thundering towards me through the hidden pathways.

'Bea! There you are!' shouts Isa, jogging along and waving at me as she spots me.

'Hiya, Bea!' calls Mags. 'Where is my Schubert? Where is my Bertie?'

I raise my hand to wave back at Isa, but before I can speak to respond to Mags, Schubert and Bertie cease their frolicking and run (or waddle fast/buzz speedily) towards the little girl.

'Mow wow!' shouts Schubert in delight.

'Bzz bzz!' echoes Bertie. Mags is just about the only other person he speaks to — or at least the only other person who understands him — apart from Nessa — so he's beside himself with joy.

'Didn't interrupt anything, did we?' asks Isa, with a suspicious glimmer in her eye.

'Not at all,' I respond.

'Hmm. I'll find out. Schubert will tell me,' says Isa, and I kind of believe that's true which makes me flush again.

'No, it's all good,' adds Marcus. 'All good.'

Is it? I want to ask. Is it really? Because I'm a mistake, aren't I? But I choose not to descend to such petty levels when I have two curious girls standing so close to me.

'Schubert found the key to the gates,' I offer instead. 'Look — they're open.'

'Wow! Amazing!' cries Isa.

'Amazing!' says Mags.

'Just in time for the Honey Festival,' adds Isa.

'Festival,' repeats Mags.

I forget that sometimes these two are a double act.

'What are you doing here, anyway?' I ask. 'I thought your dad was coming to get Schubert.'

'Ah, he is. But we were passing on the bus, so we got off and decided to come and see you. We'll just wait for Dad.' Isa is already texting Scott, Nessa's oldest brother, fingers flying across the screen of her phone. 'Can we go in the summerhouse with your Spell Book, please? While we're waiting?'

'Waiting.'

'Yes — that's fine. Just be careful,' I tell them.

It's the same thing I tell them all the time and Isa rolls her eyes. 'Aye. Careful.'

'Careful.' Mags does a mini-eye roll and I bite my lip to stop myself from smiling. I don't envy Scott and Liza dealing with these two.

'We'll stick to making something nice. Probably with lavender and chamomile in,' says Isa decisively. 'Uncle Hugo and Aunty Isla say it really helps Harris sleep.' Hugo is yet another of Alfie's brothers. 'They like to rub his feet with the cream we made him. Weird.' She shakes her head. 'Babies are weird. You were a weird baby, Maggie.'

'Weird,' says Mags and shakes her head too. 'Come on, Schubert. Come on, Bertie. Let's go!' She does her Warrior Princess stance where she raises her arm commandingly, and I can imagine her with a trident or a big stick leading an army of elves. But in this case, she turns smartly on her heel and begins to march towards the summerhouse.

'Spell Book?' asks Marcus.

'Yep.' I watch the four of them head along another path, Isa humouring Mags by letting her go in front and swinging her arms as she strides along behind her. 'The summerhouse is the big wooden workshop building where I let them make lotions and potions, and the Spell Book is basically a herbalist's recipe book. It used to live in the Visitors' Hut with me, but since these two have been coming more regularly, I just decided to leave it there. Don't worry — it's harmless stuff they make.'

'You're really good with them.' Marcus sounds impressed. 'With the girls, I mean.'

'They're good kids. Isa is helping with my Honey Festival advertising and Mags is drawing pictures.' I realise we have sort of deliberately moved away from discussing The Mistake, and I don't wish to dwell on the issue myself, so I feel it's a good time to draw this little liaison to a close and send Marcus on his way. 'Okay — well, thank you for letting me in the potting shed, and for being there when Schubert found the key.'

There's a beat, and I see a flash of something cross Marcus' face, which might be a little bit of regret, or a little bit of relief that I'm not mentioning anything about what happened between us. 'Thank you for being there too,' he says. 'And for helping me open the gates.'

We both look behind us at the gateway, still wide open and inviting, and it makes me shiver. It was a beautiful moment, but it can't go any further. I mean, realistically, I'm still banned from entering the Glentavish gardens — and as a guest of The Man, technically, I suppose, Marcus shouldn't be here, in my Garden, either. They are two different worlds.

'You'd best go,' I tell him. 'Remember to lock up behind you.' That sounds quite ironic, as it's been locked for decades, hasn't it? And oddly I feel a bit like crying and stamping my feet instead of laughing or breezily waving him off. 'Thanks again.'

'Yeah. Thanks.' He stands a bit awkwardly and looks at the key in his hand. 'Do you . . . ?' He lifts it up.

'No thanks.' I shake my head. 'You take it. It seems as if it belongs to Glentavish House. You need to take it back there. At least I know where it is if I ever need it.' Not that I'll be asking Banshee Carla or The Man for it any time soon, I want to add.

'Okay. I'll pass the trug and things back for you. Pointless you having to clamber across the wall when we've got a nice gateway now.'

'Pointless,' I say, nodding.

I feel like Mags, repeating his words.

'Yeah, I'll not be around much after this weekend, anyway,' he says. 'I've got a new series I'm filming, so I'll be in Islington for a few weeks. I don't think I'll be back for your Festival, so I'm sorry about that . . .'

'No need to be sorry. Even better reason for you to leave the key in the potting shed. I definitely won't be needing it, and neither will anyone else.'

'It is a bit pointless,' he agrees. 'You having it here, I mean.'

'Pointless,' I mutter again. As far as I'm concerned, that is the end of the conversation.

I fold my arms and hug myself as he walks over to the gateway and brings my things back through it.

The gates close, with him on the other side, and I hear the gentle clunk as he locks them up again.

It feels horribly like an ending, rather than a beginning.

* * *

That was just one of the weirdest experiences of my life. There we were, having a fantastic time, and I almost kissed her. I almost bloody kissed Bea! What am I doing? It would be so unfair to get into a relationship with her — or indeed anyone — at the moment. Work is manic, and I'm barely here, so how could I ask Bea to commit to a long-distance relationship?

The last time I did that, with Rachel, it didn't end well at all and I felt guilty for weeks. Rachel had every right to break things off. I was the most unreliable boyfriend she'd ever had, she told me — in a very cool, polite way, because that's what she's like. Rachel said that if a couple are in a relationship, they should give each other a decent amount of attention and it just wasn't working for her. She wasn't wrong. But, actually, she didn't thank me for then pointing out that, as per her relationship preferences, that if one half of the couple happen to be "from the Television" (I even waggled my fingers in a hipster sort of way to denote speechmarks around the phrase), then "the Television" (more finger waggling) probably had to take up a large part of that person's life. To retain the status quo, kind of thing.

After I said that, I swear that if looks could kill, I would be a corpse now.

To be fair to Rachel, she wasn't wrong about the attention thing. I did miss and/or cancel quite a few dates, and even Carla pointed out that fact. However, Carla was, oddly, more on my side — "you're right to want to build your brand," she'd said on more than one occasion. "That's what'll count in the future." I used to agree with her enthusiastically to stop myself from feeling too bad about the whole thing. So maybe, upon reflection, I should cut her some more slack on the "brand" thing with Glentavish. Perhaps she thinks I'm still of the same opinion? And like I say, at some undetermined time in the future, I'll do something more practical with the outbuildings. There's no need for me to keep them all to myself, is there? I'm only one person, after all.

One thing I do know, though, is that I still don't think it was right to let that almost-kiss happen with Bea. The last thing I want to do is lead her on. Especially when the true identity of The Man is still unknown to her. I can only blame the magic seeping around us from that Garden and the excitement of finding the gates.

Very dishonourable, Marcus Rainton. Very dishonourable indeed.

Even the fact that Bea and I managed to open the gates has paled in comparison to how guilty I feel, and it was really horrible closing them back up again; with Bea on one side and me on the other. I wonder if she's upset with me — maybe she'll deliberately plant some fast-growing plants up the gates on her side to block out the view of Glentavish House, instead of having it all opened up with the view straight down as Lady Clemmie wished.

And now I feel disloyal to Lady Clemmie for ruining her daydreams.

Gah! The woman died over a hundred years ago! I'm just being melancholic and stupid now.

It's all — yes — pointless.

I stomp my way back up to the potting shed, seeing the piles of bindweed and greenery we pulled out earlier. I need to bag it up and bin it; I can't leave that lying around. Carla will do her ends and I definitely can't deal with that.

'It'll spoil her clean lines,' I mutter to myself, and kick a small stone out of the way in temper. The idea of cutting Carla some slack didn't last as long as it should have, then — my bad. But this is different, because the "clean lines" thing affects Bea. Not me.

I hang the key back up on the wall, on a convenient nail, and remember Bea and I walking through that gateway together, laughing. Such a small thing, but it's taken on a whole load of significance in my mind.

Oh well. I walk purposefully back up to the house. I'll start making dinner. Spaghetti Bolognese. Simple and nice, and yes, it'll be a treat for Carla coming in. She's basically house-sharing at the minute, so it's just as easy to cook enough for two of us as it is to cater for myself.

See. I'm cutting her some slack.

My phone beeps again, and I take it out of my pocket and read the message.

Okay.

Yep.

Drinks turned into food. See you later. C x

I shrug, and then type: *OK. Enjoy. Will make spag bol and keep some back for you if you want supper. M x.*

She doesn't answer, and I'm not surprised. Like I say, she's building a social life up here, and I'm not one to stop her meeting friends. Spag bol for one it is. But I shouldn't complain. That's the way I want it, right? No relationships. No one to share my cooking with.

Just me. On my own.

Later, after I've showered and changed and washed some of my strange mood away, I scroll through my phone as I'm waiting for the spaghetti to boil. I find that the Facebook page for Bea's Garden has been updated, just this afternoon.

Not long until our amazing Honey Festival! Come along and sample sweet treats and all things honey. Buzz along on the second weekend in August! "Bee" great to see you!

Accompanying the post is a picture of Schubert, with Bertie (I assume it's Bertie) on his nose, with the cat looking at the bee in a cross-eyed fashion. They are posed in front of a beehive, with two more hives in soft focus behind them. Next to them is a pile of small glass pots, with the words "Hunny Creem" handwritten on the labels. One or two of the labels have crossings out on them, and I can't help but smile. Obviously, Isa and Mags have been busier this afternoon than just making potions.

I click "like" on the post, even though I know I can't make it because of my work commitments.

But maybe, after what's happened today, that's a good thing?

CHAPTER NINE

Bea

Marcus and I have a complicated relationship, I have decided. Well, I think we have a complicated relationship. I clearly like him, and I think he likes me, and heaven knows I've stalked him quite a lot. By that, I mean I've watched many, many episodes of Hidden Architecture. It's a good show, and also a great way to hear his voice and look at his face. I still keep thinking about the way we almost-kissed. And the way we broke through the gates, which feels as if it should be awfully symbolic — but maybe I'm overthinking. Maybe he doesn't "like" me as such, and almost-kissing me really was a mistake?

Like I say, it's complicated and it's scrambling my brain thinking about it, so I decide to do something else.

I decide to do some more research on Lady Clementine. I decide to do this after watching Marcus on TV, after he'd helped a family find the outline of a bathing pool in their mahoosive garden — much, much further south than we are, so it was clearly warmer down there — and he also helped them find old plans which showed it was actually fed by the sea, so it was tidal, and they restored it and everything.

There were some final shots of their three blonde mop-pet children splashing around in it, and it made me think of Lady Clemmie, and how she'd had three children in three years. There was a much more sensible gap between the mop-pet children than a year between each of them, but I'm sure it was still like herding kittens. Isa and Maggie are enough for me, and only in small doses — but I guess if they're your own children, it's easier than if they're someone else's.

I don't know.

What I do know is there is probably quite a bit I can find out online, anyway, so I pull my laptop over, pour a glass of wine, and keep Marcus on in the background on catch-up. It's crazy, but hearing his voice makes me feel happy, almost as if he's in the room with me. I suspect he doesn't feel that way about me, but I'm allowed to have a little crush on a celebrity, aren't I? Millions of people do.

However, it kind of makes me feel like I'm no better than a screaming groupie, so I turn my attention to Lady Clementine Eliza Grey and dig into as much of her history as I can.

Marcus is correct. She came to Glentavish House with her new husband, Sir Archie Robert Grey, at the tender age of twenty-one. She was what they delicately class as an "inva-lid", and yes, her world was probably quite small. I have visions of her flopping around on a chaise longue all day languorously towards the end — probably coughing a lot with consumption. But she still managed to have three chil-dren — Hamish, Rose and Robert — even though she died after having Robert; very, very sad, but quite usual in those days, I guess.

Throughout their brief marriage, Lord Archie, bless his cotton socks, (or bless his pantaloons — did they wear socks in those days?) built her a drawing room, and a salon, and a sitting room, and he was in the process of planning the Temple to the Four Winds she so desperately wanted when she died. Obviously, it seems it never got built; I imagine that Lord Archie was so distraught that it just never happened.

I look at the plans — because it's amazing what you can find on a library website in digitised form — and it's beautiful. What really resonates with me, though, is that there looks to be a sculpture of a little beehive on the top of it — and I immediately feel another sort of kinship with Lady Clemmie.

What makes me even more excited is that I've also managed to find the paintings online from Glentavish House; the ones Marcus described. They must have been added to some online collection, and her picture is definitely based on that sketch from the local history booklet as far as I can tell. I stare at Clemmie for a while. Marcus is correct — she was very pretty with curly brown hair and big brown eyes that even managed to twinkle with mischief out of the frame. Her husband was a good-looking chap too. Fair-haired with blue eyes that had a matching twinkle in them — and then, suddenly, I feel really sad.

'I'm so sorry it ended for you both like that,' I say to the picture of Clemmie on the screen. 'I'm so sorry you didn't get your Temple to the Four Winds — but I am pleased we managed to clear those gates for you, so if you are lingering around Glentavish House, you can have a look out of the window and see straight down here again. It's not perfect, but it's all I can offer at the minute.' I think back to when I fell into the Glentavish gardens that first time, dressed in my bumble bee outfit, and I wonder again if the ghosts I sensed around me then, in that grand old house and those neglected gardens, included Clemmie.

I bet they did.

I stare at the portrait for a little while longer, and realise I'm in danger of becoming maudlin — I am two glasses of wine down right now — so quickly switch off.

I must occupy my mind with happier thoughts. I must think of the Honey Festival and see what else I need to sort out. I only have a couple of weeks, and I know there's not much to do, but it does give me a sense of satisfaction to see what's been sorted and to plan out where everybody's going to be situated in my head.

I open my trusty spreadsheet, followed by my "Vital List" document and finally I access the shared folder which Isa set up for us to all use; me, Fae, Tavey and Isa herself. There are copies of emails in neatly labelled folders within the shared folder; photos are in there too, and copies of all the important documentation I need. Tavey has even put a list of allergens in the folder for the cakes and bakes her Whisk and Waffle group are going to provide. It's looking fantastic, and very, very organised.

Isa will do well in her IT exam, I think. She's even sorted my website out, which is all super-modern and mobile phone friendly now.

I smile as I look upon my Honey Festival folder, and my smile grows wider as I can see Fae is in there too — her little icon has popped up in the corner of the Vital List and something has just turned from amber to green, so I know she's now finished working with Pippa to finalise details of the coffee cart arriving.

I decide a little chat on the messenger service might be nice, then we both decide a video call would be better, and I have my third glass of wine and Fae has her second gin cocktail while we chat — and I can truly push thoughts of Marcus and our complicated relationship to one side . . .

But I admit that would be a lot easier to do if he wasn't still talking to me in that rich, smiley, chocolatey voice from the corner of my lounge.

* * *

Marcus

I'm in my flat in Islington, having finished filming an episode of Hidden Architecture in a Victorian cottage in Kingston. Tomorrow, I'm at a Georgian mansion house in Kensington. I tell you, a person gets to see all sorts of places in this job, and I do love it.

But this time, it's different.

I really enjoyed being shown around the neat little garden in Kingston, and demonstrating that there had been a second property attached to the cottage, and that's why the property had two staircases. Last week, I was in a tiny cottage in the Cotswolds, knocking down a wall to discover a tiny hidden staircase; that's the theme of the bumper episode coming up — staircases. And I am looking forward to seeing the mansion house tomorrow too, and maybe finding more stairs . . . but my heart is still in Glentavish.

Glentavish House has three staircases: a sweeping main set, a servants' set and a pretty little set with shallow steps leading up into what used to be Lady Clemmie's private wing. The staircases were definitely one of the things that attracted me to the House when I first saw it. But normally I don't feel as much of a pull to the place as I have been feeling today.

I don't know if it's because I'm thinking about the fact we've now opened up the space between the two pieces of land, and it all just seems brighter and like progress has been made, or if it's something more; whether the thing that's pulling me back is more to do with Bea, and the time we shared there.

I've never felt that I wanted to be at Glentavish House so much before; Carla would probably prefer me to stay away anyway, so I don't interrupt her project — and sometimes I have found myself doing just that. She just doesn't seem particularly happy about me being around when she's trying to work. I do often hope that the renovations uncover some hidden gems at Glentavish, though. But, as yet, we have found nothing.

Except the gates into Bea's Garden, of course . . .

Do they count?

Of course they do.

This weekend coming, I was intending to stay in London, due to the fact I'm filming again next week — but then I'd briefly wondered about a fleeting visit to Glentavish. However, I've missed a couple of calls from Carla over the last couple of weeks, and then shortly after the last one, I got a text telling me not to worry about this weekend, not to call back, and it was probably best not to return to Glentavish anyway, as "people will be taking over the place". I guess she means the electricians and the damp-proofers. Anyway, it's best if I stay away, apparently. I haven't argued, because I have plenty to be doing down here.

But then it suddenly dawns on me that this weekend is also Bea's Honey Festival. I've seen so many staircases and stairwells these last couple of weeks that the time has just flown. Ironically, the Honey Festival is something I did want to go to, but I'm not sure I'd be particularly welcome there anyway, after the way I left things with us — although I'm sure that it will be a fun event.

If I could go to Glentavish this weekend — if I could — I would be going more for the Festival than to check on Carla's project . . .

Oh, what a tangled web we weave.

I think about the last part of that quote, where it goes on that we practise to deceive or something.

I'm actually not deceiving anyone though, am I? I'm staying away from Bea because I'm worried that the feelings I've started to develop for her are just a bit intense. It's not fair to anyone if I'm thinking stuff like that, given how busy I am and how much of a mess I made of the whole Rachel situation.

It's difficult to get my head around.

I think, if I'm deceiving anyone, I'm deceiving myself. But the jury is out on what I'm actually deceiving myself over . . .

My thoughts are interrupted by my mobile phone beeping. In capital letters, Carla demands that I ANSWER THE BLOODY PHONE MARCUS. And then it starts ringing, making me jump. I see her name pop up on the screen. Maybe those missed calls over the last fortnight have been more urgent than I thought — if she's ringing again, there must be a damn good reason for it, and my stomach clenches a little. Is it her? Is it the house? Has something happened?

Because it doesn't seem as if it's going to be a simple "hello, how are you?" call.

'Hello, Carla!' I say, trying to placate her before she speaks. 'It's nice to hear from you. How's—'

'Marcus, that bloody cat is in the house. It's in the house! Covered in bloody honey! And . . . and . . . it's rampaging! For fuck's sake, it's mad! It's bloody mad! Can you hear it! Marcus! What are you going to do about it? It's spoiling everything! Marcus! Marcus? Bloody stupid, big, fat, stupid, rampaging, stupid, bloody cat!'

My lips are moving but I find I am unable to formulate words. There's too much in that garbled speech to unpick, but I have to force myself to tune into something and respond to that bit at least.

'Can you get Bea to come and get him? He probably won't respond to you and you'll just put his back up if you shout at him—'

'We are way beyond me shouting at him,' rages Carla. And, indeed, I can hear a joyful mow wow-ing coming down the line. 'I mean, there are people here — important people. I've got the press here taking pics and—'

'The press?' It's my turn to raise my voice. 'What the hell have you got the press there for?' I look around for my car keys, as if I'm going to jump in my car and drive all the way up there to chuck them out of Glentavish House this minute. 'I mean, I know you said there'd be people around this weekend—'

She cuts me off. 'Because they're doing a local news piece, and they asked if they could come to see what the place looked like and talk about future plans. But that's beside the point. The point is that cat is here, it's broken into the house, and it's rampaging!'

The point for me is that the press are in my house and I knew nothing about it. But it's not productive arguing about it now. When I next go home, I'm going to have to have a proper talk with Carla. This can't go on. It really can't. If I'm being pedantic about it, I'm paying Carla to do a job, and then there's stuff going on — like reporters — that she doesn't even run by me first.

It sounds like the place is going to be swarming with the press as well as the workmen this weekend!

'Okay. Look, I have the number for Bea's place — it's on my annual pass. Give me a moment and I'll find it and you can call her.'

'I'm not calling anyone,' shouts Carla. 'You do it. You ring her. It's her fault — hers and yours. You should never have cleared that stupid gate. That cat's been in the grounds loads. I keep seeing it and chasing it away, and it must be using that ridiculous little entrance to come and go—'

'Carla! Stop it. Okay. I'll call her.' Good grief. 'I'll text you when I've rung her. Just . . . just try to contain him in one room or something. Bye for now.'

I hang up and quickly dig out the annual pass. I know I wanted an excuse to talk to Bea again — a valid excuse — but this wasn't what I'd planned on.

But still. It has to be done.

So I do it.

* * *

Bea

It's a couple of days before the Honey Festival and I feel pretty on top of things. We're collecting and bottling the last of the honey, and because Isa and Maggie are grumpy and bored as they approach the end of their school holidays, I've allowed them to help.

It was slightly against my better judgement — if you recall, a few weeks ago I was adamant that I wasn't going to allow Isa anywhere near this job. But I've been supervising them the whole time as Fae has been manning the Visitors' Hut, and very helpfully handing out leaflets about the Festival and drumming up some extra trade.

Well — I say Isa and Mags were being supervised the whole time, and this is where the problem has arisen. I had to go and speak to someone who wanted to hire the summer-house for a botanical arts and crafts session, so left the girls and Schubert — and Bertie — alone for ten minutes.

Ten minutes.

And that's all it took.

I've just finished speaking to the potential customer when the phone rings in the Hut.

I look at the phone in surprise. Not many people call it, and it's doubly unusual that someone should call it when I'm in the Hut. Usually, I just respond to an answerphone message and call the person back.

'Hello, Bea's Garden!' I say brightly.

'Bea? Is that you?' I almost drop the phone at the sound of the voice. It is so very familiar, yet so very unexpected. It's familiar because I've heard it coming out of my TV rather a lot recently. Unexpected, because: why would he ring me?

'Marcus?'

'Yes — yes, it is. Bea, I'm so sorry to ring you, but I didn't know what else to do. Carla has just called me, and from what I can gather, Schubert is . . . rampaging around Glentavish House. Covered in honey.'

'What?' I shriek. 'Impossible! I just saw him ten minutes ago. He was with Isa and Maggie and Bertie. They were all by the beehives and — and — and . . .'

And nothing.

It's not impossible at all.

In fact, it's eminently possible that Schubert has indeed rolled around in honey and pelted across my Garden to use his cat-gate, and then continued to pelt up to Glentavish House.

I mean, he's a large cat and there's a lot of him to propel, but I have seen him run when a tin of tuna or salmon is being opened fifty metres away and he thinks he's going to miss out. He becomes Usain Bolt Cat.

'Tuna,' I say stupidly. 'Or salmon. Was there tuna or salmon involved?'

There is a beat — unsurprisingly so — and then Marcus says: 'Tuna? Salmon? I don't know, Bea.'

I shake my head to try and see some sense in it all. 'Forget it. Forget the tuna and salmon. Okay. I assume tuna and salmon have nothing to do with him in his rampaging or honey-covered capacity.'

'No. Not at all. Can you do anything about it? I'm in Islington . . .'

'I'll see. I'll see if Isa and Mags will go and get him. I'm not setting foot in that garden. Not when Carla or The Man might be around.'

'It's just Carla,' says Marcus sounding contrite. 'Look, Bea—'

'No, it's okay. I'll sort it. Leave it with me. Goodbye, Marcus. Thanks for letting me know.'

I don't even wait for him to respond before I hang up and clatter the phone back into the cradle, then I run outside. 'Schubert alert!' I yell at Fae, who's drifting around with a watering can near a trellis covered in rambling roses. 'I have to go and sort it out. Sorry, Fae! Can you look after things here? I'll not be long.'

I don't wait for an answer and run towards the beehives, where Mags gazes up at me. She looks adorable with a daisy-chain crown on, but I can tell it's contrived, especially as Isa is wearing one too and looking far too innocent. And yes — even Bertie has a tiny daisy flower balanced on his head. Unbelievable. The three of them are in cahoots. I can just tell.

'Oh oh,' little Maggie says. 'Oops-a-daisy. Schubert ran away. Dearie me.'

'Maggie, sweetheart,' I say. 'And Isa. And Bertie — yes, you Bertie. What on earth happened? We need to get him back. He's rampaging!'

'Well, now.' Isa thinks for a moment, looking into the far distance. Then she wags her finger irritatingly in the direction of Glentavish House. 'The story we got from Bertie there, was that there were some intruders in the Big House, and Schubert clearly decided to investigate.'

'Intruders?' I'm confused.

'Yes. Some pooparazzi or something.'

'Poop,' says Maggie. 'Pooparazzi.'

I ignore her. 'But what are paparazzi doing there? At Glentavish House?'

'Well, they aren't actually pooping—'

'Pooping.'

'—it turns out they were just journalists from the local rag.' Isa shrugs. 'So the paparazzi weren't there. Not really. But by then, Schubert had dashed through that honeycomb there—'

'—and he slipped and rolled,' adds Maggie.

'—and he slipped and rolled,' agrees Isa. 'And then he picked himself up again, and slipped again.'

'Oops-a-daisy.'

'Oops-a-daisy. And then he was off.' Isa points towards the gate and wags her finger. 'Like an Olympic athlete.'

''lympic.'

'But he's rampaging!' I say pathetically. 'Rampaging!'

'Bertie says he doesn't like Carla,' says Maggie. 'No, no, he doesn't.'

I look helplessly at Bertie, and via a shifty little buzz he confirms it.

'That's no reason for him to be over there causing chaos. We need to get him back. And I can't go, so one of you will have to.' I look at the three of them. 'Now!' It's my turn to point angrily at Glentavish House.

The girls look at one another, and I think if they do "rock, paper, scissors" to decide I'll shout at someone.

Then, surprisingly, Maggie stands up and brushes grass from her chubby little tanned legs. 'I'll go,' she says. 'I'll use Schubert's special gate.'

'Maggie!' She seriously means to crawl through that gate?

Then she creeps me out a little by blinking and looking at me way too innocently. 'I have done it before. I fit.'

'I'll come too,' says Isa. She's a skinny, wiry, flexible teenager and yes, I suspect she can fit through that cat-gate as well. Schubert can do it and he's not a small animal. 'We'll not be long. Bertie?'

'Bzz bzz,' he agrees, and before I know it, the three of them are running (or flying) over to the gate, and then, somehow, they're all on the other side.

I see them pick up speed and run (or fly) towards the house. And all I can think about after that is the state Schubert will be in, if he's covered in honey and whatever else, organic or non-organic, he has collected on his travels.

Then my phone beeps.

Shall I prepare the sink with a gentle floral bubble bath? asks Fae. He'll let me bathe him. Not a problem x

I can't believe this. I really can't. How and when did my life get so surreal?

Yes, I text back. *Please do x*

* * *

Marcus

I hang up and stare at the phone. I have absolutely no idea what is going on up there, and no idea whether anyone will tell me after the fallout.

I sort of expect a text from Carla saying Schubert has been removed. And I sort of don't expect a message from Bea saying the same thing. I mean, why would she tell me? I was passing a message on. She will have dealt with it. End of.

I think, though, I know who I'd rather hear from.

This can't go on. I have to sort it out. And sort my feelings out, as well. And I have to have a very long and difficult conversation with Carla about boundaries. Press people at Glentavish! Unreal!

I exhale. I feel pretty nervous about that conversation with Carla. She's not the easiest of people to reason with, especially if she thinks she's doing the right thing. But I can't say any of the things I want to say to her — to either of them, really — over the phone or via text message. Because I know I also have to tell Bea the truth about my connection to Glentavish House. It's gone on far too long, and I've been thwarted every time I've tried to talk to her about it.

There's nothing for it.

After the filming for the Georgian property in Kensington is wrapped up, I need to head back there. I'll shelve everything else for a few days.

I need to head home to Glentavish House.

CHAPTER TEN

Bea

The forecast is looking good for the Honey Festival tomorrow. At least, that's what Fae tells me and I'm not going to argue with her. We've got our stalls sorted, and the traders are going to come first thing in the morning. Then, of course, we have the little coffee cart coming as well, which I'm really excited about. Pippa has asked if she can come quite early to set up. We're due to open at nine, so that sounds splendid to me.

I'm feeling a little bit fizzy as I go to bed. The Honey Festival is always a lovely day, and this is our fourth one so we should sort of know what we're doing by now. I've been bottling honey for days, and that's without counting the Schubert Rampage Day because I prefer to forget about that, thank you very much. Isa, Mags and Bertie brought him back safely, but not one of them — not one of them — looked regretful.

However, those stickers that Fae organised are almost all used up, and the honey jars certainly look the part. It's been a good harvest, and my bees still have enough honey in the hives to keep them plump and happy throughout the winter.

Poor Bertie doesn't know if he's coming or going. He's my man on the inside, and he's being really helpful, but he's got a lot of fellow bees to keep in check. He's doing a splendid job, though. I think he's trying to make up for Rampage Day. He'd got the bees trained enough to huddle to one side of the hive while I collected the last trays of golden, drippy honeycomb to work with. I mean, I can only imagine how annoying it must be if a giant comes in and lifts an entire floor of your house out through your roof . . .

It's this I ponder as I climb into bed. Oddly — or maybe not so oddly, means as I have been consumed with honey-ness for weeks — I dream about being a honey bee and buzzing around Marcus' head to get his attention. I haven't seen him for a little while, but that's understandable, I suppose. I haven't heard from him either — not since Rampage Day — but that's possibly a good thing, as I don't want any more calls about Schubert misbehaving. And Marcus has got a job to do, after all. I still have no idea what his cousin is like, and don't want to know, and I binned the latest note that came from the place without opening it. But Marcus and I did find that key!

I'm not sure what The Man might think about me having access to his grounds though. Horror of horrors, he might use the gate himself to stomp through and challenge me about my fronds . . . or that awful Carla might come through, uninvited.

But I refuse to think about Carla and The Man.

Instead, I think about Bertie and my Garden and Marcus. And my dreams are very pleasant in the end.

* * *

Marcus

It's the night before Bea's Honey Festival.

My job is finished in Kensington, and I've decided that I'm definitely going home.

I find I can't wait to get there, so I'm intending on travelling up very early. I'll get a plane to Edinburgh if I can, rent a car from there to save a bit of time, and I'll see Bea in person. But before that, I need to speak to Carla.

Which won't be so pleasant, and sets a bit of a dark cloud over the coming day . . .

* * *

Bea

It's the day of the Honey Festival! I'm super excited — so excited that I'm out of bed and dressed and driving to work at seven o'clock.

But by seven-thirty, my good mood and excitement totally evaporates.

The Garden car park is full.

Full to the brim.

There's no room for the coffee van, or traders, or visitors or anything.

'What the hell?' I jump out of my car at the gate, not even able to access the car park myself, and look around in vain for someone to ask.

'Bzzzz. Bzzzzzz.' Bertie appears and starts dive-bombing each car in agitation, as if he can move them by force of his tiny will alone.

'Bertie, sweetie, stop it, darling,' I call. 'They're bigger than you.' I mean, bless him, he stops and he comes over to me and sits on my shoulder, his tiny body vibrating with indignation.

I hear the sound of an engine coming up behind me, and I turn to see Pippa's coffee van pulling up. My heart starts pounding and I feel a little sick. This is the start of it — this is my first trader needing a space.

Not to mention that I'm in great need of one of Pippa's full-bodied coffees right now.

Then I hear a very familiar clip, clop, clip, clop. Fae comes up behind Pippa, driving her Apothecary's Cart with Roger the horse. A black, whiskery, furry face is squashed up against her — Schubert, of course — and Alfie is there too, blinking owlishly behind his spectacles and looking bemused.

Fae draws Roger to a halt. Roger looks sleepily around for some handy vegetation to eat, and Fae speaks. 'Is there a problem, Cousin Bea? Because it's rather early and you might need some caffeine to kickstart your mind because we kind of need to be in there — oh. You do need caffeine. Right.' She nods.

'I need more than caffeine.' I wave apologetically to Pippa who has parked up nearby, and hurry over to Fae. I suspect she can see over the top of Pippa's van from her vantage point, but just in case she's unsure of the full epic failure of this morning, I feel the need to share something obvious: 'The car park is full. We can't get in.'

'That's rather an issue,' says Fae. She turns to Alfie. 'I'm so sorry for getting you up so early. I didn't anticipate this.' She blushes and I avert my gaze. Nope, I'm fairly sure that if Alfie stayed over with Fae then there were other things on her mind than just the Honey Festival.

'And Schubert?' I ask. 'I'm not certain he anticipated getting up so early either.'

'Mow wow.'

'He didn't.'

'And Roger?'

'Neigh.'

'He's okay with it.'

'Hmm.' I nod. 'Fae, I'm panicking a little.' I wave my arm in the direction of the full car park. 'Pippa's here, and it won't be long before the others arrive either.'

'I say!' A pink Volkswagen Beetle pulls up behind Fae, and I recognise the cheerful voice of Tavey through the open window of the car. Roger whinnies a greeting — he sees in Tavey a kindred spirit, as she is quite possibly the "horsiest" person we know and definitely has an affinity with the equine population. 'I wanted to set up our Whisk and Waffle stall and marquee early, just so we're all in place. Have we got a problem?'

I groan and sit down cross-legged on the ground, my head in my hands.

'Bit of a queue!' calls another driver, as I see the wheels of another van pull up behind Tavey.

This is not an auspicious day.

'Oh God, oh God, oh God . . .' I mutter.

Soon, there are quite a few cars and vans forming a queue. I check my watch. We have less than an hour before the Honey Festival opens.

There's a scuffle from Fae's cart and Schubert slithers out of his seat. He's sort of squished himself between Fae's knees towards the bit of wood that sticks up that she rests her feet on — no, I don't know what it's called — and done that thing where he seems to make himself into a long, thin sausage, which truly has to be seen to be believed, and he's managed to slide past Fae and flop out of the cart and form an untidy heap on the floor. He de-sausages himself, shakes himself, and stalks off purposefully towards my recycling bins. When Schubert stalks purposefully, it's more of a directed waddle. I stand up and watch his hindquarters swaying as he disappears, and then I turn back to Fae, who's looking a little surprised that Schubert has managed to squeeze past her.

'I don't even know who all these people can be,' I say. 'Sometimes the ramblers park up but they always tell me, and they don't do it when I have anything big on.'

'I don't think they're ramblers.' Fae looks over towards Glentavish House. 'I have rather an odd feeling about that place today.' She jabs her forefinger in the direction of the estate. Alfie shrinks back in his seat to avoid Fae's finger sticking in his eye as she's very close to the rim of his spectacles. He pushes them onto his nose more securely and says nothing.

'The Man?' I look at Fae. 'He wouldn't sabotage my Honey Festival, would he?'

'Mow wow.' I look down at my feet. Schubert's comment is muffled yet self-righteous, and he has a crumpled-up piece of paper in his mouth. I don't give too much thought to the speed at which he extricated that piece of paper from the recycling bin, or how quickly he came back to us.

Instead, I lean down and take the slightly soggy document from his whiskery mouth. 'Thank you,' I tell him, and he nods regally. I understand that I need to uncrumple this piece of paper and read it.

And when I do, my heart sinks into my tummy and my jaw drops open in horror.

* * *

Marcus

There's something so peaceful about driving through the countryside early in the morning. It's already quite warm so I hope the Honey Festival is a great event for Bea. I feel that I really do need to support my neighbour — even though she still doesn't know I am her neighbour.

I suppose I could be surprising Bea in more ways than one by turning up. Probably Carla as well. I texted her, but the message came up as "undelivered" so I can only assume she's got her phone off. I suppose she did tell me that she'd be busy this weekend, presumably with workmen, so it's unsurprising.

My stomach does a little lurch. I really am going to have to come clean with Bea and have a stern conversation with my Project Manager — but I did find that key, so I'm hoping that Bea, at least, will forgive me. Maybe I can say I bought Glentavish House from my cousin, or something. That's one way around it.

Well. Okay. I know that's the coward's way out, but I think that if Bea knows it's not me who's been complaining about the plants, and it's all been a big misunderstanding, ha ha ha, then it might be all right.

I can hope anyway.

I mean, I haven't known Bea long, but I've noticed her eyes go a really odd shade of gooseberry-green when she's angry and it's pretty scary.

116

My mind drifts to how pretty she is normally, and then I squash down on my drifting mind as I can't let myself fall for her as much as my soul seems to want to.

Carla, however, a little voice seems to be saying to me, has fallen for Glentavish House big time. I think she could chuck me out with the rubble she's had workmen shift from the outhouses and never give me a backward glance.

I think again how lucky it was that Bea's cousin's boyfriend's sister's cat got stuck in that old potting shed — I mean, talk about six levels of separation and Fate and all that malarkey. I shake my head wonderingly. Life can be very strange at times.

But hang on — what's going on here? The road to Glentavish House seems blocked, and there are a shedload of vans and things in a queue with people out of their vehicles and peering along the road, and what looks like the back end of a Gypsy caravan up front.

I pull up at the end and get out of my car. 'Hey, sorry to bother you,' I say to a woman standing next to a small floral camper van. 'What's the hold up?'

'I think there's a problem with access to the car park at the Garden,' she says. 'I'm here with my honey skincare products, and I was hoping to be all set up for it opening.' She pulls a face. 'Poor Bea. I bet she's frantic.'

I look along the queue and I can see Bea just next to the Gypsy caravan — yes, there she is — and Schubert is next to her with something in his mouth. She leans down and takes it from him, and then she unfolds it.

And I'm not kidding — her face changes on the spot from worried and anxious to full on hell-cat. Her head snaps up and she looks around wildly.

Even at this distance, I know her eyes will have that terrifying gooseberry-glow to them . . .

As her gaze swings around, it settles on me — I'm not kidding, even stuck here at the back, she homes in on me like a hawk spotting its prey.

'You!' She suddenly yells. 'You! How dare you! How dare you?'

I sense the question is rhetorical — largely because I have no idea what I'm supposed to have done.

Yet.

I mean, she doesn't know I own Glentavish House yet . . . does she?

'You own Glentavish House!' she screams, waving the paper in her hand at me and beginning to stomp past the queuing vehicles.

Okay. I guess she does know I own Glentavish House.

I quail.

I've been in some crazy situations before with work, but never have I faced anyone who looks as furious as Bea Appleton does right at this moment.

'Bea.' I step towards her. 'What's up?'

'So you're not denying it then, are you? Are you? You're The Man. The Man! The Man who wants me to chop all my plants down for his bloody clean lines. Well, I'm not surprised that you started hacking back at that bindweed. You didn't even know it was a weed, so I bet that was going to be on your list for me to hack off next, was it? Were you just pretending to help me clear the gates so you could keep chopping back at stuff? And to not tell me! To not tell me who you were—'

'It's Marcus Rainton,' comes a helpful voice from a pink Beetle up front.

'I know. Thank you, Tavey. I know. I know exactly who this person is — this, this charlatan . . .'

I wonder whether Bea is ever going to run out of breath or shouty-voiceness, and I wince; it doesn't seem like it's going to happen any time soon.

'Bea, look. I was going to tell you. I was—'

'Forget it,' she hisses. 'Just forget it. Forget it and make it right, you awful, awful . . . Man.'

I can hear the capital "M". I can literally hear it.

I reach out to take her arm, to guide her away from the queue of traffic, conscious that everyone is now looking curiously at us. Thankfully, none of these people seem the sort to be recording Bea's outrage on their mobile phones and uploading it to their social media, but it's still not pleasant. Bea shakes my hand off and raises herself to her full height.

I mean, she's magnificent, absolutely magnificent — but God almighty, she's bloody scary. And I was right about her eyes. They are now mesmerising in their gooseberry-ness.

'Okay, you're right about me owning the house, but I swear I haven't been sending you any letters,' I say. 'And I'm guessing you only just found out — because you're really being quite scary, Bea — so I suggest we kind of move away from the crowds and talk about it more quietly?'

Bea waves the piece of paper in her hand at me again. 'You did this. You made people park in my car park, in the Garden's car park, on my Honey Festival day — to run a sodding yoga retreat. It's here. Here in black and white.'

She thrusts the paper at me, and I stare at her, uncomprehending. Automatically, I take the paper from her and smooth it out.

What I read makes me feel sick. Sick, and angry — angry at Carla.

GLENTAVISH HOUSE YOGA RETREAT
Come and experience the tranquillity of Glentavish House, the Scottish home of Marcus Rainton, for a two-day yoga retreat, facilitated by instructors Carla Dobbins and Eduardo Spirelli.

Connect with yourself in our purpose-built studio for two days of self-care and wellbeing. Sun Salute with us on the eastern lawn. Explore the grounds at your leisure and come together for an extended session of music and gentle stretches on Saturday evening.

Self-catering only, no accommodation on-site, but feel free to camp in our grounds, or sleep under the stars.

Free car parking available at the nearby Bea's Garden car park, just a few hundred yards away — we will have no vehicles on-site, so we don't spoil the essence of our retreat.

Only £200 per person. Non-refundable.

And the date, of course, was today.

Written beneath the details, in Carla's distinctive hand, was a note: Aware the dates clash with your Honey Festival. You may need to arrange alternative parking for your visitors. Your car park is common land — we've checked — so we felt we should let you know, out of courtesy, that it might get quite busy. Regards, Carla and Marcus.

I wasn't quite sure what I was most angry about. Top of my list was quite possibly the suggestion I'd been a party to all of this. Closely followed by the fact Carla had gone ahead with this without telling me. Also, the fact that that strangers were on my property, in my garden, camping and stuff. The fact that Carla had chosen a date that I was meant to be working away for. That she'd charged people for it — who was getting that money? The fact that Eduardo Spirelli, her mate from her yoga classes, was part of it.

And, obviously, the fact that Carla had deliberately sabotaged Bea's big event of the year and told her people to use the Garden's car park.

The list in my head went on and on and on.

And all those "we's" in the letter — making it look like we'd both arranged this and agreed to this. Or, God forbid, that we were a "we". As in a couple.

I'm not surprised that Bea's infuriated.

I'm infuriated myself.

'You,' hisses Bea, and I look up from the flyer into her furious face. 'You are The Man. And you never said!'

She's not going to let that drop, is she?

'Like I said, none of the problems you've had with Carla have been anything to do with me. And that includes this letter and this yoga retreat. I was supposed to be away this week, working. I wasn't supposed to come back until Monday—'

'So you could stay out of the way and plead ignorance and blame that cousin you invented? To stay on my good side?'

'No! Not at all. Look. I was genuinely meant to be away. All I know about yoga retreats and people visiting for courses is that Carla wanted to make a business of it at Glentavish House. I told her there was no way the place was ready for anything like that, even if I wanted to go down that route, but she clearly decided to do it anyway. When I wasn't around. Bea, I'm going to sort this out.' I wave my hand at the queue of traffic and at the car park. 'I'm going to go up there and have it out with her.'

'Well, you can't drive up there, can you? Because the road is blocked with my traders for my Festival because your yoga people are parked in my car park!'

A little voice rings out from quite near the front of the queue. 'Roger can scuttle. He doesn't have to drive on the road and can use the ditches and fields to walk in. Would you like to borrow Roger to get there quicker?'

I'm not sure how to respond, but I eventually go with: 'Ummm, no thanks. I'll walk.' I'm assuming Roger is the horse.

I shove the flyer in my pocket and turn around. I decide to jog rather than walk — this needs to be dealt with pretty quickly.

'Mow wow.' Even Schubert, it seems, is urging me onwards. I have no idea where he is, but his voice rings out.

I jog faster.

CHAPTER ELEVEN

Bea

'Unbelievable!' I shout at Marcus' retreating back 'You are unbelievable!'

I stomp a few paces after him, half-wondering if I need to make a point of following him, but I decide not to. Largely because I need to be here, telling my visitors that they can't get into my site.

Quickly, I assess the verges — I wonder if it's at all possible to begin setting up on the side of the road. It might be possible, but it's still going to cause some traffic issues, and will the visitors really want to park half a mile down the road to buy some honey? From past experience, they want to see the Garden as well — it all adds to the enjoyment.

I groan. It's doable, just not what I want for my Honey Festival — yet all these people, all these little businesses, have taken time out of their day to come here and make other people happy. And over the wall, there are a shedload of people all going "ommmmmm" in the gardens, and thinking it's perfectly above board that they can use the Garden car park. On a normal day, it would be annoying; but on a day like today, it's downright disrespectful that Carla and Marcus have allowed this.

And I thought Marcus was nice! I thought he was a sort of friend, I guess — a supportive person who helped me get the gates cleared, and found a key for me, and everything . . .

And someone who almost kissed me, which adds a whole new layer of hideousness to this — because it looks like Carla is his girlfriend, and not The Man's? That makes it so much worse!

Bertie comes and sits on the top of my head, and we both stare along the lane after Marcus' retreating personage. He's quite a way in the distance now.

I bet he can't maintain that jog all the way around. I've walked that distance in a bee costume, and it's tough.

'Mow wow.' I look down and feel Schubert lean against me and crush my legs at the same time. I think he's being considerate and sympathetic — and maybe a little sorry that he found that letter and caused a shouting match so early in the morning.

'Oh, it's not your fault, sweetie,' I tell him, sighing. I rub the fur between his ears and he makes what I think is a deep, throaty purr, which sounds more like a chainsaw. 'At least I know now. We can deal with Marcus and his untruths at a later date; we just need to sort this parking and Festival rubbish out first.' My stomach does churn and clench a bit. I honestly didn't think he was capable of doing this. I don't want to think he is capable of this.

'I'm not sure he is.' I look up and Fae has done that thing where she just kind of appears silently next to you and hovers. Okay, she doesn't really hover, but she might as well be hovering.

She's also doing that thing where she reads my mind.

'"Something is rotten in the state of Denmark",' she quotes, which surprises me as I didn't think Fae was into Shakespeare—

'Nope, I love Midsummer Night's Dream. You can keep Hamlet though. They all die. But there is something rotten here.'

Okay.

'Definitely an odour of corruption.' She wrinkles her nose. Right at that moment, Schubert breaks wind un-embarrassedly. Yep. I agree with her.

'But I honestly think it's Carla. I don't think it's Marcus,' she clarifies.

'Mow wow.'

'You too, Schubert?' I look down at him, still unwilling to believe that Marcus was capable of such a devious trick, but feeling that the evidence is irrefutable.

'Mow wow.'

And then, strangely, Bertie comments. 'Bzz bzz.'

Bertie usually keeps his opinion to himself, so it makes me think that if Fae and Schubert and Bertie, of all creatures, are in agreement, perhaps I should be giving Marcus a little benefit of the doubt.

'But he did lie. He led me to believe it was a random cousin that owned the Big House. He was very, very vague about that.' I purse my lips because that bit is definitely something to rake over with him at a later date.

And he almost kissed me!

'Yes, Cousin Bea. I agree. But our immediate issue is the Honey Festival. We've still got a little time — I have every faith that this will work out well.'

And if Fae has faith in that, I should probably believe her.

'Mow wow.'

'Bzz bzz.'

I'm outnumbered. I guess I just have to wait it out and see what transpires, but I'm not the best at inaction and part of me is twitching desperately to do something and stay busy, piling honey jars up on a table for sale or digging in the Garden. I suppose that's why Bertie and I get along so well. We understand one another.

But it seems as if this one is out of my hands, so I'd better be prepared to stand at the end of the queue of traffic and explain the problems to everyone who turns up until we know what's happening.

* * *

Marcus

I eventually reach the gate to my property — my property — and I can hear a weird noise coming from the other side of it.

It's like a strange drumming, and voices that sound as if they're going "omm omm ommm".

As I go through the gate and head towards the house, I see some tents pitched on the lawn — and a portaloo standing to the side. What the heck?

I speed up and see some people in a group doing some sort of position that makes them look like human pretzels. A pale, slightly effeminate young man in skin-tight exercise gear is at the front of the group, leading them in what I guess is some sort of routine. This must be Eduardo, then.

Just along from there, in front of what used to be the stables, is a group of people drumming and chanting. Random yogis are wandering around; some of them are lying on the grass, reading or relaxing — and I have to hand it to her: Carla certainly has a lot of people here. Which also explains the rammed car park at Bea's Garden.

And at two hundred quid a pop, she's no doubt made a lot of money from the weekend. But it's not the money I'm bothered about — it's more that she's done all of this behind my back and deliberately, it seems, to derail Bea's Honey Festival.

And I need to find her.

Thankfully, as I reach the front door, there's a sign marked Private on it. At least nobody will be hanging around the house. Except, hopefully, the person I need to see.

'Carla?' I push open the door and look around. The house is much as I left it a couple of weeks ago, which is rather surreal I have to say. I walk through the building until I get to the area she claimed as her office, and barge in without knocking . . .

Okaaaaaaay — that guy in the skin-tight clothing was not Eduardo then, because Eduardo, I assume, is actually the lean, toned and very manly Mediterranean-looking guy who's currently forming a human pretzel shape with my Project Manager. If I thought for a brief moment there might be a gentle way of discussing the boundaries of the project in relation to the boundaries of Carla's management of the project, I am now of the opinion that there is definitely no way back — after all, who wants to walk in on their employee making like a pretzel with a yoga instructor in the actual environs of the project?

Not me.

'Carla!' I snap. 'I think we need a conversation about all of this, don't you?'

'Marcus!' She springs apart from Eduardo. 'What are you doing here?'

'I live here, remember?' My voice rises in anger. 'This happens to be my house, but it seems to have turned into a yoga retreat!' I look at Eduardo. 'With a hint of brothel.' I glare at Carla again. 'Carla, what the hell are you playing at?'

'I told you I was interested in yoga retreats! I even said I'd run one as a taster, and you would have nothing to worry about and wouldn't need to get involved with it — but you were so engrossed in pandering to that stupid girl over the wall that you clearly didn't listen to me!' She opens her mouth to say more, but I'm not prepared to listen. Again, it seems.

Instead, I tell her, 'You said you'd think about doing a yoga retreat "at some point" if I was happy about it, Carla. And come on, I know that attack is the best form of defence. There's no way any of this should have happened here without my say so. Was this why you rushed through that barn conversion? It wasn't about getting it sorted as a project for your portfolio, was it? It was always going to be used for — this.' I wave my hand in the general direction of the gardens. 'And was that why the press were here? To drum up some publicity for you?'

'You have to diversify your stream of income,' she shouts. 'Have different ways of making money—'

'And whose income stream are you talking about? Because I'm pretty sure I never wrote a business plan to make this place into your yoga retreat! And maybe, just maybe, I might have come around to the idea "at some point",' I shout back, echoing her words, 'but to come home and find you did it without telling me is just wrong. It's wrong, Carla. You were helping me out. We were meant to be working together, and this happens?'

'I thought you said your boss was happy to accommodate us?' chips in Eduardo. To give him his due, he does look a little astonished. As well he might, having been caught in a human-pretzel shape with someone.

'Hmm. And that's where you're wrong.' I glare at Carla. 'Her boss is not happy to accommodate it. I mean, I might have been, at some far distant point in the future. But not now. And certainly not by deliberately disrupting Bea's Honey Festival. And definitely not by letting you do — this — in my house.'

Surprisingly, she doesn't even have a response for that one. She just looks at us, from one to the other, and I think she knows she's beaten. Then suddenly her mouth turns down at the edges and she actually looks a little more human, and a little more vulnerable, and a little more like the Carla I originally knew.

'You just don't get it, do you?' Carla says. 'I was really excited about this project. It was ideal. You could do so much here, and I was willing to help you make the most of it. But you're just not interested. I don't even know why you bought this place. You never come here, you don't have any opinions. You just keep telling me to get on with it. So I do, and you don't say anything. Despite what you think, I did mention it, loads of times, and you didn't disagree, so yes. I pushed it, okay?'

I open my mouth to respond, and one of our many conversations about retreats flies into my mind: "I'd run a session as a taster, and you would be safe in the knowledge that I had it all under control. You wouldn't have to lift a finger. In fact, you wouldn't need to be involved at all."

"Sounds good to me."

Bloody hell!

And another . . .

"Did you fancy doing an art retreat?"

"Oh no. I was just looking. Yoga's my preference."

"Yes, yoga's more your thing, I guess."

And yet another . . .

"I could make some money in an instant by organising a retreat. You should let me. It would be great exposure. For us both. I need to futureproof myself as well, you know?"

"Well, maybe at some point."

Good grief. This is awful! And as the remembered conversations are making me go hot and cold all over, Carla is continuing to speak. 'I wanted to see how far I could go, whether it could be something I could do in the future. That stupid TV programme wrecked my career, because Feenix brought us all down with her — and I'll admit this . . . project got out of control. We'd been talking about retreats at yoga, and all of a sudden I realised I had something. I could do this. And I did it. Because I could. And also because you gave the impression you'd let me. Because let's face it, you don't care about anything else at the moment, do you? You're more invested in that stupid wall and that stupid Garden next door. I hoped that if you saw what an amazing job I was doing with Glentavish, and how I could bring more money in, by working with you, renting the studio from you or something, it would all work out. This retreat was a good idea. A great idea, in fact. And the car park is common land. I'm perfectly entitled to let guests know they can use it.'

I try to ignore the ghosts of those conversations, and respond. 'It might be a good idea. It might even be a great idea,

Carla. But not now! In the future, like I said. And certainly not on the date you chose. Deliberately, I suppose, as well?'

Carla tosses her hair back and looks defiant. Also, she looks a bit as if she's about to cry. 'Of course it was deliberate. You were away. I wanted to make a point and I wanted to warn that woman off. Because I can tell you like her, and I hate that fucking cat. And yes. Maybe I hoped that eventually I could stay here on a more permanent basis — that perhaps, at some point, you'd see what a great team you and I make at Glentavish, and that, maybe . . . we'd even get together.'

Wow. She just said that next to the person she was pret-zelling with!

Actually, he's still smiling, so maybe he's cool with that . . . !

And I don't see what the issue is with Schubert — I mean, apart from the rampaging thing . . .

I bring my thoughts back to the conversation at hand: 'But who's getting the money from the retreat?' I ask, trying not to look too much at Eduardo.

'Aaah, that would be myself and Carla,' chips in Eduardo, still beaming. 'Is good, yes? A good income for very little effort. See, we will plough it back into our next event which will be bigger and better!'

I just stare at Carla.

Sadly, she had made some decent points before Eduardo helpfully commented — but then she had already spoiled it, right at the end, when she mentioned she'd chosen the date deliberately and dissed Schubert. If she knows I like Bea, which she certainly seems to, she has to know that doing something like this would never endear her to me. And, actually, beneath the outrage and anger I'm feeling, I know I need to try and make this right for Bea as well. I can't ask these retreat people to leave — they've paid good money to be here, and it's not their fault. They came here in good faith.

'I'll have to let Bea's lot set up here and have the Festival at the bottom end of the lawn,' I say. 'And people can just go through the gates to visit her Garden. It's the best I can do to sort things out for her.'

I stomp through the house, pull open the front door and stare outside.

'These people have paid for peace and quiet!' Carla yells after me. 'You'll be going against everything they've paid for!'

I swing around, furious. 'Then give them their money back,' I fire at her.

There's no answer from her, although I can almost sense her fizzing and bubbling with anger, because she knows I'm right. To my mind, I'm about to diversify their experience — what could be nicer than free access to Bea's Garden and a Honey Festival at the bottom end of the place you're relaxing in? The grounds are big enough to share, and it's what we're going to have to do today.

I stomp outside, and . . .

'Mow wow?'

'Bzz bzz.'

I look down in surprise, and there is Schubert the cat looking quizzical, with a bumble bee sitting on the top of his head between his ears. I suspect he's a lot cleaner and fluffier now that he's not rampaging around covered in honey.

'Hello,' I find myself saying. I hunker down in front of the animals, a fairly mad idea breaking into my mind. 'Could you take a message to Bea, please?' I ask, quite politely, because instinctively I know politeness is everything when you ask a cat to do you a favour — and a bumble bee, I guess. 'Let me just nip back in, get some paper and write it down, and then you can run back with it — if you don't mind? I'll go and tell the yogi guys, if you let Bea know that people can start driving up the lane and come into the grounds.'

It's an extraordinarily long shot, but I have a feeling it will work. And time is of the essence right now. It really is.

'Mow wow.'

'Bzz bzz.'

I think they really do understand.

* * *

130

'Have faith,' murmurs Fae serenely as we stand helplessly along-side the growing queue of cars. 'Have faith.' Pippa has very kindly started to dish coffees out, and I've already drained mine.

I think it's an odd thing for her to say, so I chew the corner of my thumbnail anxiously and stay silent.

'Ah-ha,' she says after a few minutes. 'Look. Look, Cousin Bea. It's Schubert and Bertie!'

I look down and, sure enough, Schubert is there. He sits down in front of me and stares up, fixing me with his eyes. There's a folded-up piece of paper in his mouth, and I assume he wants me to take it from him.

'Bzz bzz,' affirms Bertie, who is apparently along for the ride.

'Okay . . . May I? Thank you.' I remove the paper and reflect how this is so much better than the gift of a dead mouse might be.

'Not pleasant,' mutters Fae.

I ignore her and unfold the note.

I read it, then read it again.

I look up at Fae. 'We have to direct everyone up to the Big House. Our Honey Festival is relocating.'

'What? Amongst the retreat thing?'

'Yes. He — The Man — Marcus — says he'll unlock the gates in the walled garden. The traders can set up at the bottom of his lawn, and they can park in his grounds towards the right of the house so it doesn't disturb the yogis.' I feel a little huffed that the yogis aren't to be inconvenienced, but then the better part of me — the honey-sweet part of me — understands it's not their fault. They paid their two hundred quid in good faith, after all.

'It's very kind of him, I suppose,' I say stiffly, 'but he still allowed it to go ahead—'

'Mow wow!'

'Bzz bzz!'

'Not at all!'

131

I'm a little taken aback. It seems as if my companions disagree and are sticking up for him.

'Carla did it.'

'Mow wow.'

I look to my best friend, little Bertie, who would never ever lie to me for final validation. 'Bzz bzzzzzzz,' he tells me seriously.

'Okay. It was all Carla—' I begin.

'It was.'

So I need to revisit this later; quash it down, give Marcus The Man the benefit of the doubt, and, first and foremost, get my traders out of this awful queue and up the lane, right into Glentavish House's grounds.

'Come on,' I say to Fae. 'Let's pass the message on.'

'I'll get Alfie — oh. Hello, Alfie.'

Alfie has suddenly appeared next to us, still looking a little bemused. 'I thought you might, ummm, need . . .' His voice peters out and he shrugs, confused, seemingly wondering why he's actually wandered over here.

Alfie is very much like Fae in many ways. I pat his arm. 'Yes, Alfie. We need you to help us. We need to get all these cars and vans to head up the lane. If the three of us—'

'Mow wow.'

'—four of us.'

'Bzz bzz.'

'—five of us can go to the traders and let them know what they need to do — that's head up the lane, Alfie, and drive into the grounds of the Big House, then set up there — we can start directing visitors too. Actually — is it okay if I run to the Visitors' Hut? I can make a sign and put it at the entrance to the car park . . .' My mind is racing ahead, but fortunately everyone seems to understand and four heads (even Bertie's) nod in agreement.

They scatter and begin to speak to people in the queue. Schubert and Bertie stick with Alfie, clearly to give him some moral support, but soon I can see vehicles beginning to move off and up the lane.

I turn and run towards the Hut. There's that old chalk-board I can use to make the sign and that should work well, I think.

It only takes me a moment to locate it. I turn it around and see the chalk drawing of a cat and a bee on the back, sitting either side of a honey pot (a "hunny pott") and grin at Maggie's artwork. I hesitate for a moment, wondering if I should rub it off and write on a blank board, but then I smile and instead write the message above and below the image.

Bea's Garden "Hunny" Festival.
Please park at Glentavish House.
See the traders in the estate, then visit the walled garden through the newly discovered Victorian Gateway.

Then I pick up the board and scurry back to the car park. I prop it up at the entrance and stand with my hands on my hips, watching the slow-moving vehicles snaking up the lane towards the Big House.

I decide to run back to the Garden, just to make sure access is clear from our new gateway into next door's garden. Candybelle Bubblegum lives in that border after all, and she's notorious for thrusting her blowsy pink flowers at anyone who crosses her path. She's a beautiful hydrangea arborescens and the bees love her, but my goodness she can be a madam if she wants to be. It's the time of year where she's at her provocative best, so I know she'll need to wind her beautiful neck in to let people through and stop hogging the limelight.

I shall have to have a word with her.

I run up to the border and, sure enough, she's quivering with excitement with all her blooms pointing eagerly to the gates.

'Hey, Belle,' I call. 'We might be getting a few people coming through here today. Now I know you're gorgeous and everything, but we've got to be kind, yes? Let them through and don't block them, or we'll have a pile up.'

I rest my hand lightly on one of her branches and I think we understand one another.

Beyond Belle, the usual suspects of honeysuckle and ivy and rambling roses and jasmine are framing the gateway, and I can't help smiling. It'll be such a treat for visitors to walk through the gates and for those beautiful scents to tickle their noses.

'Bertie,' I say, looking around me. I know he's here somewhere; I can hear him buzzing. He's probably flitting around Belle. 'Can you get the guys to kind of stay away from here for a bit? People sometimes flinch if they see too many bees.'

There's an indignant buzz, but then he agrees.

'Thanks, Bertie.' I turn my attention to the gates and put my hands on my hips. I haven't actually considered how I'm going to open these, as there's only the one key — and unless Marcus—

I catch my breath. There's an inexplicable shift in atmosphere, a shadow darkens the gateway and the Garden does that thing where it all goes silent . . .

There's a click, and the handle turns. The plants around me crowd in and form a soft, green, earthy canopy, protecting me and hiding me from the outside world. Then he opens the gates and there's nothing between us but the width of the wall.

* * *

Marcus

'Bea!' I stop, my hand still on the handle, halfway through the wall. 'Wow. Well. This could be awkward.'

'How?' she asks. Her hands are on her hips and she stares up at me. Her voice is harsh, as it might well be expected to be, but it's also a little wobbly, and I think I know how she feels. I think we might just have snatched victory from the jaws of defeat as far as her Honey Festival is concerned, but the fact Carla had ulterior motives is still taking a little time to process. 'How will this be awkward?' Bea persists. 'Is the awkward part the part where I have another go at you and Miss Yoga Fiend in there, because you've tried to wreck the one event of the year that brings the Garden a nice chunk of income?'

'It's awkward because I'm stuck in a gap in the wall, and if I leave go of the gate it'll slam shut, but if I step into your Garden to prop the gates open, you might have a go at me. Oh. Hang on. You just did have a go at me. Fancy that.'

'Well, can you blame me, Marcus?' She throws her hands up in the air and shakes her head. 'What does it look like? I get a letter like that, and it's signed by both of you—'

'Allegedly signed.'

'Okay, allegedly signed by both of you, and it really does look as if you've done this deliberately. You were my friend. Or at least I thought you were. And you lied to me. You lied to me about being The Man, and made up a cousin who you led me to believe was The Man — and all that time it was you! And you were in a relationship with that Banshee!'

'I was not in a relationship with Carla. Let me make that absolutely clear, Bea. And it wasn't me who was trying to spoil things. It was all her. I admit that I do own the house, but it never seemed I ever had a chance to tell you. Every time I tried, something happened and I couldn't. But please believe me, I never wrote any of those letters. Please Bea, please believe me. I don't know an aspidistra from an apple blossom. I wouldn't know what was invasive and frondy and what was short and stumpy. I mean, what's that? Is it a rhododendron?' I point to something pink and huge, and Bea glares at me.

'She is called Candybelle Bubblegum, and she's a hydrangea. Belle for short.' Bea's expression changes as she looks affectionately at this ball of pink petals, smiling at it indulgently. The pink thing quivers and wobbles, and I blink.

It must be the wind.

'The point is,' I say, dragging my attention away from the ginormous flowerhead, 'that it would serve no purpose for me to wreck your Garden or your Honey Festival. Carla is the one who has been driving this yoga retreat thing, and I must say she's gone and done all of it behind my back. Oh, and by the way, if it makes you feel better, she was pretzelled around a man called Eduardo when I went in the office, and I walked right in on it.' I blink, seeing it again in my mind. I shudder. 'I think he's Italian.' As if that makes a difference! They're both pretty flexible, I'll give them that.

'Well, that can't have been pleasant, walking in on them. I mean . . .' She pulls a face for a second, obviously imagining it. 'Look, Marcus the Man, I'm having a bit of a stressful day.' Her eyes suddenly drift downwards. 'Munstead, sweetie, thank you, but even you can't calm me down right now.'

I follow her gaze, and, leaning softly against her legs, are some stems with silvery-grey foliage and deep purpley-blue flowers tickling her bare skin. I'm not kidding — they are actually tickling her; I can see them stroking her gently like tiny fingers. I watch, fascinated. I'm not even sure that lavender bush was there earlier.

'Like I say, I'm stressed. I can't be worrying about your girlfriend, or your non-girlfriend—'

'Non-girlfriend.'

'She told me she was your partner. The first time I saw her. She said my "partner" owns this place. She actually did say that. Partner.'

'Business partner.'

'Whatever. I can't be worrying about her doing downward dog with a random Italian bloke. This is my Honey Festival. And although I'm super-pleased and thankful to you for letting my traders use your estate, I'm still a bit cross, Marcus, and I need to get today out of the way before I can think about anything else. And that includes sympathising with you. Which I don't, by the way, because I really dislike Carla and she's a nasty piece of work, and I think you deserve a better Project Manager—' She clamps her lips shut, but my ears do prick up at that.

Then something buzzes, very close to said ears, and I duck instinctively.

'Bertie. Come on, we've had a conversation about behaviour today, haven't we?' Bea — the human Bea — addresses her comments to the bee that's flitting around, and then she holds her hand out, palm upwards. The bee buzzes once more, a little indignantly, I think, and lands on her hand. Then it lies down.

Bea looks at me, a little challenge in her eyes. 'My best friend is a bee, and I talk to plants. What do I know about you doing better?' she says. 'If that woman isn't your girlfriend, you obviously chose to work with her, and kept working with her. You clearly gave her free reign. This is pretty much all on you. So — anyway — thanks again for letting people park in your grounds and come through the gates into my Garden. The rest of all of this is a conversation we need to pick up again—not the conversation about you doing better with your choices, though,' she adds hurriedly as I open my mouth to comment. I close my mouth again. 'But we do need to talk about what's been going on and why you lied to me.'

Having said her piece, she nods briefly and turns away. Then she pushes through a bunch of plants that seem as if they have all crowded in a little more to find out what's going on; and then the foliage sort of closes up behind her, leaving me standing in that cocoon of fresh greenery. A little shiver runs up my spine and I look around. Then the plants curl away again, and it's suddenly a clear passage through from my garden to Bea's Garden.

It's weird, but I feel like I'm being judged by a whole load of plants. Or Nature Spirits?

There's a rustle in the leaves which may or may not be the wind in the branches, but I'm not hanging around to find out.

Quickly, I latch the gates open, attaching the hooks to the rings on the back of the wall, and hurry back through to the grounds of Glentavish House. It's only as I stand in my garden that I feel I can breathe again and my heart stops pounding quite so much.

137

CHAPTER TWELVE

Bea

I think, I actually dare to think, that we've snatched victory from the jaws of defeat. I'm standing next to Pippa, a takeaway coffee cup in my hands, watching the visitors walk through the gates and into the Garden, having enjoyed some stalls at the Honey Festival in the grounds of Glentavish House.

We decided that Pippa would be best placed here, so customers walk in and immediately spy a nice place to buy coffee, and it's worked well. She's been rushed off her feet and is joining me in a cuppa for a few moments of downtime.

'Didn't you say Tavey had brought some flapjacks? I think a flapjack would go nicely with this,' Pippa remarks.

'She's got some traybakes she's experimented with.'

'Oh. A traybake would be nice.'

'Lemon and courgette traybake.'

Pippa's top lip curls. 'Oh.'

We watch the visitors in silence, and I notice that Pippa makes no attempt to go and find Tavey and her traybakes.

'There's just something,' she says after a few moments, 'about a vegetable in a cake.'

'Carrot cake,' I offer.

'Always an exception to the rule.'

She still makes no attempt, and I must say I don't blame her. It could be the nicest traybake in the world — but once Tavey has added her individual stamp to it, I don't think it's quite the same any more.

'I think, though, that the visitors seem to be enjoying the event,' says Pippa, sipping her latte.

'Yes. Roger's been a huge hit, Fae has doled out loads of advice, and the girls are doing well with their lotions and potions.' I smile in the direction of a small camping table that Isa and Maggie have set up. They're selling their "creem" and other goodies, and they are dressed identically in little yellow peasant-style tops and cut-off jeans and yellow sandals. They've both got their red hair tied back in bunches too and I have never seen Isa look so damn innocent.

Schubert is under the table as well. I did see Nessa earlier, so I assume she's come to take him home, but he's currently relaxing after a constitutional. Nobody is looking for him at the moment anyway, so I guess he's where he's supposed to be, which is always good news as far as Schubert is concerned, because you never can tell.

At least he's not in the compost heap or rampaging around covered in honey today.

'If we made them dress alike, they'd freak out.' Liza — Isa and Maggie's mum — comes up to the side of us and nods at her daughters. 'But no — if they want to do it, they'll do it.'

'I love your girls,' I say with a smile. 'I know there's a big age gap, but they are lovely together.'

'Hmm,' says Liza. 'To be fair, I'm pleased in some ways it's not any smaller. Isa was a handful growing up anyway. I don't think I could have tossed a Maggie May in the mix and stayed sane.' She laughs and hands over some money. 'Anyway, I'm here for two cappuccinos, please. Scott's over there somewhere.' She points towards Tavey's Whisk and Waffle stall. 'He says he needs something to take the taste away.'

'Understandable.'

Pippa is already making the coffees, and she smiles as she hands them over to Liza.

'Thank you!' says Liza and heads off to see Scott, who is looking both furious and distrustful of the half-eaten tray-bake in his hand.

Three children run past with balloons and pinwheels and the parents follow, the mum reading the label on the jar of honey she's bought, the dad more interested in the mead he's carrying, holding it like it's a delicate prize.

They catch our eye as they walk past and smile. 'We've had a great day, thank you,' says the woman. 'It was so nice to park up at that house and walk through the gardens. You should expand and take over that place as well. Imagine how amazing it would be!'

'Ah, I don't own that estate,' I say, smiling back. 'But it's been an experience, finding the gateway between them and clearing it all up.'

'Yes, we noticed that was all new since we last came. It's fantastic. Thanks again. We'll be back!'

'I'm so pleased,' I tell them. 'Oh, some people are so lovely!' I say as they move on and I turn to Pippa.

'They are,' she replies. Then she looks at me a little slyly. 'I'm sure some people can be even lovelier if they're given another chance.'

I hold my hand up to stop her talking, because I know exactly where she's going with this one. 'Someday, perhaps. Not today. Today, I'm cross and flustered and have other things to think about.'

'I don't think you're that cross and flustered now, are you?' asks Pippa. 'It's all worked out beautifully, don't you think?'

'Hmmm,' I say and refuse to engage any further. Instead, I pay attention to Bertie. He's buzzing around delightedly, having a good look at what people are doing and participating as much as he can.

He zips over to Isa and Maggie, and Maggie looks up and catches sight of him. She grins and he zooms around her head, buzzing close to her ears, then he finally settles on the top of her head.

'What's that mean then?' Pippa is following my gaze. 'In bee folklore.'

'Ahh, it means she's got to expect a happy and successful life,' I say. 'That's what it means if they buzz around a child's head. Also, I think he's whispering secrets to her. Someone must have told him something exciting. Bertie is no good with restraint.'

'Good old Bertie,' replies Pippa. 'Is he coming with you on your holidays?'

It's perhaps a random thing for someone to ask, but I've known Pippa forever. I'm having two weeks' holiday after the Festival — ten days with my family, and a few days visiting her. She's a good friend and Bertie is always welcome.

'Not this time. He's going to chill out here for a bit, I think. But yes. Good old Bertie.' I drain my coffee, give Pippa a quick, thankful hug, and head out on my own constitutional to enjoy the Honey Festival.

* * *

Marcus

I need to make this up to Bea. I watch the last of the cars pulling away from the temporary car park at Glentavish, and then head down to the gates to lock them up.

I must admit, it feels good to be taking back a bit of control. I think I am to blame for this a bit, to be honest. Bea's voice comes back to haunt me: "This is pretty much all on you." I mean, I know my name is on that leaflet, so it looks pretty bad to an outsider like Bea — but then again, what was I to expect? I knew it wouldn't be pretty when she found out. I just wish it had been in a less public way, and that the situation we faced today hadn't happened. But I got so caught up in work that I just let Carla power on, and wasn't interested enough, or just around enough, to appreciate what was happening at Glentavish. Maybe she did try to talk to me. Maybe she took my silence as consent, or maybe she chose to deliberately misunderstand.

If I think about it long enough and re-process some of our conversations yet again . . . well, I can see where she might have thought I was happy for her to do this. But she's never known when to stop, and I can well believe that it got out of control.

Or maybe she was just worried about the project finishing, losing her job in TV, and made some poor decisions to try and protect herself for the future? And if she'd chosen a different day for her retreat, I might not have reacted as badly as I did.

It was the mere fact it was a deliberate choice to get back at Bea for whatever reason.

Well, I'll definitely have to sort out some boundaries, and not be so consumed with work that I lose focus of my real life. This debacle just proves it. And I think the more time I spend up here, the more I'll be able to step back, find myself again — so I know that I'm really just Marcus and not Marcus-Rainton-from-the-Television — and enjoy Glentavish. I mean, the gardens are amazing, and could be even more amazing if they were looked after and restored properly.

I know that I'll have to allow this current retreat to go ahead, but no more. At least, I think, unbending slightly, no more until a good length of time has elapsed and everybody has had time to breathe. I'll also have to see what else Carla's got hidden under the other tarps that have popped up over the old stables since I was last here. I can't let something like this happen again.

And depending on how things go, I may also need to employ a new project manager. Carla's done a great job with a lot of the project — I can't take that away from her — but there's having a sense of pride in your job, and then there's having a sense of misplaced ownership and, yes, several ulterior motives. We are the same people we've always been, and she's never been interested in me before — although I suppose I didn't own a Scottish mansion before . . .

And that may indeed be what's changed her opinion.

I need to take a good long look at what's really happening with Glentavish, and now I've stumbled upon this extra-curricular project of Carla's, it'll be a heck of a lot easier to make my case for her to reassess things and think properly about her future.

We definitely need to sort it out. She needs to step away and I need to step up. I'm not an unreasonable person, so I'll let her use whatever she needs to create her CV and portfolio; she's done a ton of work, after all. But it's been to her specifications, not mine. And I think that will be what she needs to reign in if she ends up doing this as a career. She'll have to work with the clients' wishes, not her own.

Or maybe she'll just go down the yoga route. Who knows?

I'll have to tell her she can't stay on-site any more for a start — but I'll help her find somewhere local to rent. I'm certainly not about to throw her out onto the street as well as everything else.

I'm unwilling to compare the two women, but I can't help it. Bea's not perfect — nobody is perfect, and I'm certainly not perfect — but Bea thinks of others. Her Garden is open for everyone to enjoy. She spends time with those two girls, and Schubert the cat, none of whom belong to her — and she seemed more upset about the Honey Festival debacle because she thought she was letting down her visitors and vendors. It wasn't simply all to do with the potential profits she might be losing.

Carla was running a non-refundable retreat on someone else's land. And goodness knows what tales she's spun Eduardo, or what promises she's made him. Regardless, between project managing and yoga, she's got two strings to her bow and her bases covered. I'm not sure which trite cliché would be best there. But I am sure that, once the dust has settled (yet another cliché), she'll make a success of whatever she wants to do. It's not my issue, really.

As Bea would say: ho hum.

I walk down to the gates with all these thoughts whizzing through my mind, and I can see Bea through the gap in the wall.

She's sitting, with her arms wrapped around her knees, her back to the gates, staring out at the Garden. It's the spot where the Temple to the Four Winds should have been.

I almost don't want to turn the key in the lock as it has that tell-tale clunk and I'm worried about disturbing her . . .

But then I realise that it's not Bea — unless she's changed out of her shorts into a white dress and dyed her hair brown since this morning. The figure turns and looks at me. Definitely not Bea.

I blink, my heart pounding, as the figure disappears.

'Thanks for today,' says a stiff little voice, hidden amongst the flowers and foliage on Bea's side of the gateway. And this voice definitely belongs to someone who has lilac hair, and who is wearing shorts, and who is not a brown-haired woman in a long white dress. 'You looked deep in thought there,' continues Bea. 'I saw you walking down and hid. I wasn't sure I wanted to talk to you — but . . . ho hum.' She shrugs and sticks her spade in the earth. 'I was just digging a bit. You know?' She indicates the patch of earth she's been clearing. 'Going to plant something here. Something meaningful. Clementine aquilegia and Eliza rosebushes. They sound perfect, but yes. Ho hum . . .'

I stare at her, and it's all I can do not to step through and take her in my arms and apologise for everything. But I hold myself back.

'Those plants sound ideal,' I say softly.

'Yes. I think they will be,' she says. I see her glance at the space where the Temple should be. 'Sometimes, I think I sense her, you know? I wasn't sure before. Just occasionally I get this weird feeling someone is watching me. But there never is.'

Her gaze lingers on the spot and I feel chills, as well as having the odd sense that someone has walked past me. I see Bea shiver as well, and the flower heads almost bow and nod, turning to face an invisible pathway that someone is walking down.

'Not so sure about that,' I say. 'Anyway. I'm pleased the Festival was a success. You deserved it. And you shouldn't have any more bother with Carla — I'm pretty sure she'll be leaving after this weekend. Even if she continues working for me, I won't be letting her live here and I'll be taking much more of an active role in the project. And you won't be bothered by The Man either.' It's a poor attempt at a joke. But now I've mentioned it, I want to continue: 'I'm sorry for all the grief he's put you through. He honestly didn't know about any of it. But he's finally learned there are more important things in life than clean lines. He's very, very sorry. And he should have been more upfront. He hopes you'll forgive him eventually.'

'Thanks. There are. And I might. Someday.' She folds her arms across her body; a classic defensive pose.

'I'm not going to apologise for almost kissing you though,' I say. 'Not at all.'

'Hmmm,' is all she says.

Conversation over, I guess.

There's an uncomfortable moment where neither of us look at the other. 'Okay. Well. I'll just lock it up then,' I say, for want of anything better.

'Actually. No,' she says softly. Then she reaches out and touches my arm gently, then quickly pulls her hand away. 'Leave it open. Just in case the yogi people want to come and wander. It's fine.'

'Are you sure?'

'Yes. I'm officially closed for a fortnight — going home to visit my family for some R & R, and then off to Pippa's for a few days. Someone might as well enjoy the place while I'm gone.'

I nod. 'Okay. I'll see you again . . . someday.'

'Someday.'

There's another horrible, horrible pause; then I nod and turn away.

I walk back up to Glentavish House with even more thoughts whirring around.

Then I suddenly stop.

I think — yes — I think I have a way to make it up to her.

My heart starts pounding, my brain clicks into gear, and before I reach the house, I have a smile on my face. I know exactly what I'm going to do.

I'm not sure it will work, but I have to try it. I have to.

CHAPTER THIRTEEN

Bea

I've had a lovely time with my family. My parents are down in Northumberland, and my brother and I tend to pitch up together to visit them. I enjoyed the beaches and the countryside down there — as well as seeing everyone of course, and then spending a few days with Pippa before I came back home. I honestly just needed to kick back and chill and be, well, looked after for a bit. That's always nice, isn't it?

I spared my family the details of the Honey Festival parking debacle, but wove an alternative tale of how the owner of the Big House had allowed us access through his grounds, and Mum thought that was very kind of him.

Little does she know how it all came about, but I'm not going to say anything to enlighten her.

So it's the first day back "on the job", as they say, and I have to admit it's good to be back. I mean, I'm sure the plants have all missed me, and Bertie definitely has, because he's super-excited when I call in to see him and the bees before heading into the Garden itself. Fae's been popping in to check on them, and he seems very happy, so I know she's done well with it.

But there's something else — an undercurrent of even more excitement than I had anticipated. But Bertie won't tell me what it is.

Instead, he makes it known that I have to follow him, and then — 'bzz bzz' — he tells me to wait, then heads into the hive and gets a load of his friends to come out as well, and it turns out that I have the best escorts in the world heralding my return to the Garden.

I'm laughing as I follow them, and we snake around the winding pathways . . . and then I see it.

I stop and stare, unable to believe my eyes.

'That wasn't there when I left!' I say, rather stupidly.

"That" turns out to be a building on the site of Clemmie's longed-for Temple to the Four Winds; which looks remarkably like, yes, you guessed it — a Temple to the Four Winds.

I stare and stare at it, my gaze roving around it, taking in the four little doors to welcome each "wind" in, and the beautiful domed hive built onto the top. There are huge holes in each side, and I think they should really house leaded glass windows — I can truly imagine those windows sparkling in the sunlight . . .

And the doors are wide open as if they're ready to welcome me in.

Bertie and his friends stream in and out, in and out, and buzz around the decorative hive gleefully. The hive appears to be completed, although the Temple itself — if that's what it is — still looks as if it needs some work doing on it.

Regardless, my gaze lingers on the bright white stonework, and then travels to the ground, where I can see newly planted flowerbeds around the Temple. I recognise the plants immediately. I was going to put them by the gates; they were the meaningful plants I talked about—

'Clementine aquilegia and Eliza rosebushes,' says a quiet voice.

I spin around and Marcus Rainton is standing there, appearing to be ready for a day in the garden; he is leaning on a spade, and looking nervous and worried and hopeful all

148

at the same time. 'I've been keeping on top of your weeds,' he says, nodding to the beds by the gates in the walled garden. 'I know they can easily get out of hand if you leave them for a week or so. And I started a little extra project too. I hope that's okay?'

I'm speechless. All I can think of to say is a garbled, 'You're wearing a white T-shirt again. It'll get filthy.'

'Maybe.' Marcus shrugs and shifts his weight to his other leg. 'But it'll come out in the wash.'

'Yes. It will. And — well — thank you. Thank you so much!'

And then to my absolute horror, I start to cry.

* * *

Marcus

Oh my God. I am absolutely horrified. I didn't expect that. I didn't mean to make her cry!

'Ummm — not the reaction I was hoping for?' I say. Shit! I've really messed up. Messed up big time! 'God, I'm so sorry. Have I messed up? I'll get it taken down. It can be removed. It's not too late. I'll—'

'No!' she squawks, tears running down her face. She wipes them away with the back of her hand and shakes her head. 'No. Not at all. I love it. I absolutely love it! Thank you — thank you so much. But you didn't have to. I mean . . . why? Why did you do it anyway? You had no need to. I . . .' Her voice peters out and she sniffs loudly.

I pass her a tissue from my pocket, and she blows her nose gratefully. I must admit, I was hoping for a bit more joy when she saw it. I'm quite confused.

'I thought you'd be more . . . joyful,' I say. 'I mean, I know it's not finished, but it'll be lovely when it's done.'

'I am! I am joyful. I am, I am. I'm just, well, over-whelmed, I guess. Nobody . . . nobody . . .' She starts to sniff again and hastily wipes her nose. She takes a deep, shuddering breath. 'Nobody has ever done anything like this for me before. It's exactly what Lady Clemmie would have wanted, I'm sure. It's her design and everything. Isn't it?'

I nod. 'Yes. Digitised plans from the library.'

'I saw them too. Digitised.' She pauses and looks at it. 'May I go in?'

'Of course you can. Like I say, it still needs some work — I did what I could. Called a few favours in. But at least it's got four walls and a roof. And the beehive is done. That was touch and go three days ago. But it looks fine now.'

'It's perfect. Do you . . . do you want to come in too?' Then she surprises me by holding out her hand, seemingly a little hesitantly, and then more confidently. 'Please.'

'I'd love to. I think I need to do some more explaining as well.' I take her hand and she gently pulls me towards her. I drop the spade with a clatter and let myself be pulled, and we walk into the Temple together.

We are surrounded by four pale green walls and the smell of plaster, paint and sawdust. I just finished the first coat of green yesterday. But Bea looks at the colour in delight and astonishment, and she doesn't even seem to see that the decorating is half-finished and needs refining a little. Well, okay. A lot.

'There will be moulded picture frames on the walls eventually. One on each side. You can decide who or what you want in them.'

She nods. 'Yes. Thank you. I'll have a think.' Then she turns slowly around and looks at the floor. It's rough and ready at the moment, but there are black and white tiles stacked up, ready to lay down in the exact honeycomb fashion Clemmie desired. And eventually, if Bea wants it, I'll organise a plasterer to come and do some fancy cornices and mouldings. 'It can be however you want it in here. It's Clemmie's floor plan, but you can decide if you want some plastering done. Fancy cornices and mouldings. Of bees. Or something.'

'And corbels or modillions,' she says in a faraway voice. 'Corbels or modillions.'

My heart is pounding and there are all sorts of feelings whizzing around my body. Feelings I've never felt with anyone before, ever.

'Whatever you want,' I tell her. I take her other hand in mine — making sure I'm not getting a handful of snotty tissue, because that would really spoil the moment — and pull her closer. 'I did it to try and make it up to you. You see, I should have told you I was The Man long before you found out. It should never have got to that point. But you really seemed to hate The Man, and I didn't want your judgement clouded — your judgement of me, I guess — and think that I really was as bad as you thought I was. It was just easier to let you think I was a nice guy, and Carla was the Project Manager for my fictitious cousin. And she wasn't someone I was employing.' My cheeks heat up. 'I totally regret that now. I regret lying to you by omission. I regret not telling you when I had the chance to. I had a few chances as well, but we'd always get distracted, or something would happen, and I never got to say the words. It was my fault about Carla. I just let her get away with doing everything she did because I didn't care enough about Glentavish. I didn't listen to her at all. I didn't appreciate what a gift Glentavish was when I bought it. My life was in London, my career came first. The house was always for the "future". I should have put the brakes on with Carla long before I did.'

'She was deceitful, though,' says Bea. 'I mean, really, really deceitful. All those letters she sent me, and that car parking thing. She didn't do nice things. So I think that some of the blame should fall on her shoulders as well. It wasn't all you.'

'It was a lot of me.'

'Okay. Well, yes.' She smiles in a watery fashion. 'It was a lot of you. But equally a lot of her. You were never unkind to me like she was. I just wish you'd told me sooner. I would have been angry and raged a bit, but I wouldn't have stayed like that for long.' She takes a deep breath. 'I like you, Marcus. I really — like — you. And I would have wanted us to be friends. I mean . . .' She looks through the huge window across to the not-so-secret-any-more gateway. It's still open and unlocked. That's how I got my crew through to build her Temple. 'We're neighbours,' she says simply. 'In fact — I'm actually on your land, if you think about it.'

'Or maybe I'm on your land,' I say.

'Maybe.'

There's a beat, and we find ourselves moving still closer to one another.

'And like I said, I don't regret almost kissing you. I mean it. I'll never regret it.'

'You said I was a mistake.'

'No — I said almost kissing you was a mistake. But that was rubbish. It was utter, utter rubbish, and I don't know who I was trying to fool. The last relationship I was in ended because I couldn't dedicate enough time to her. Rachel kept pointing out to me that it was clear my career came first, and that it was unfair to any woman to expect to be so far down my list of priorities. I didn't want to let myself fall for you, because — well — you're up here, and I'm mainly in Islington. Or Norfolk. Or Yorkshire. Or anywhere at all in the British Isles. I didn't want to start anything with you, because I was scared it would end . . .' I blink and shake my head. I'm not sure where all that came from.

'But — why did you think it would have to end?' Bea asks quietly. She looks genuinely confused. 'If you want to make something work badly enough, you make it work. I would have been happy to try and make it work. I would have been happy to fall for you. In fact, I think I did. And if it ends, it's never meant to be in the first place. But you shouldn't stop yourself from taking the risk, because you'll never do anything amazing if you don't let yourself fall just a little. I took a risk with my Garden. You took a risk by starting in Hidden Architecture. And also by getting Glentavish House. Which you got because you took a risk with Hidden Architecture.'

I think for a moment.

I think deeply whilst looking into her glorious green eyes.

And she's right.

She's definitely right.

'You're right.'

'I know I'm right,' she says.

'In fact, you're so right . . . that I really want to almost kiss you again . . .'

'I think that's a really good idea,' she whispers. 'But wouldn't it be better if you really kissed me? Like properly kissed me?'

There's a gentle breeze curling around our ankles, and a sense of warmth in the Temple which I definitely didn't feel before. And I don't think the gentle breeze is one of the Four Winds, but, strangely, I'm not scared.

And she's right again.

Of course she is.

'Bea . . .'

'Marcus . . .'

We lean into one another, my head down towards hers, her face tilted up to mine, and—

'Beaaaaaaaa! Marcuuuuuusssssssss!'

'Hey! Bea! Marcus! Are you around?'

'Mow wow!'

We snap apart and stare at one another.

'The McCreadie girls,' we both say at the same time.

Quickly, we disconnect and step out of the Temple.

Sure enough, Maggie and Isa are running towards the Temple, waving, Schubert following gamely behind.

'Cool!' yells Isa, looking at the Temple. 'It has to go on the socials.' And she raises her phone and starts clicking like a maniac.

'A beehive!' shouts Maggie, jumping up and down, clapping her hands. 'A beehive on the top! Yay Bertie!'

'He's not going to live in there,' says Isa from behind her smartphone. 'It's not a real beehive!'

'I know!' says Maggie. 'But he likes it. He told me.'

153

'Aye, and what else did he tell you?' asks Isa.

'Not saying!' says Mags and begins to caper around, Schubert at her feet.

I look at Bea, and she looks at me, and the unspoken word "later" almost whispers between us. Then we paste smiles on our faces and walk towards the girls.

CHAPTER FOURTEEN

Bea

'Hey girls!' I say, probably too brightly.

Isa snaps her head towards mine and narrows her eyes. 'Interrupting something, were we?' she asks.

'Not at all.' I am indignant.

'Hmmm. Anyway, look, we're all here. Me and Mags — we're the advanced party. The rest of the clan—' she nods over her shoulder, '—are bringing up the rear.'

'Bottom!' yells Maggie.

'Rear,' says Isa witheringly, then ignores her little sister. 'Come on — we've brought a picnic.'

'But I'm not open for another hour,' I say, wondering why on earth all the McCreadie clan have decided to land in my Garden, way too early for normal opening hours.

'And?' Isa looks at me, a cheeky challenge in her eyes. 'Bertie said it was fine.'

There's a tug on the leg of my shorts and I look down. Maggie's little heart-shaped face is staring up at me, her red curls escaping from her bunches. 'Bertie said. Is that okay, Bea?'

I sigh. 'It'll have to be. Ho hum.'

She slips her little hand in mine and pulls me towards the rest of the family group. There seem to be an enormous number of them gathered here today, lugging picnic baskets, blankets and, in Hugo's case, a chubby, dark-haired baby boy. I just know Harris' feet are going to smell exactly like lavender and chamomile, but at least he looks happy and contented about it.

I try to count the people and list them in my head. Fae and Alfie, of course. Hugo, Isla and baby Harris. Billy and Lexie. Scott and Liza. Nessa and Ewan. The whole lot of them: all of Nessa's brothers and partners. I vaguely wonder where the McCreadie parents are, and Nessa, who is passing by me just at that moment, fiddling with her mobile phone, smiles and says: 'At home. I talked to them earlier.' Then she keeps on walking.

'She's the one who showed me around Glentavish!' says Marcus, looking stunned. He points at Nessa. 'I swear it. She's from Hogarth Properties!'

'Yes. She is.' I grin.

Marcus just looks shocked, then shakes his head. 'Surreal.' Then there's a flurry of activity and Nessa's family are spreading out picnic rugs and arguing good-naturedly amongst themselves. 'This is surreal,' Marcus says again softly.

'Welcome to my world,' I say with a smile. 'I blame Fae for getting me even more involved with Nessa and her family.'

At that point, Liza looks up and her jaw drops about half a mile. She's staring at Marcus as if she can't quite believe the Marcus Rainton is in my Garden. She looks around wildly, probably for someone to share this momentous news with, and her gaze settles on Scott. I see her pull a face — yes, Liza, that's probably a little inappropriate — and I hide a smile.

Liza then homes in on Fae, who is rummaging through a huge wicker picnic basket, and she leans over to whisper something to her.

Fae looks up, responds to Liza, and then turns her attention to me. She waves, and I wave back. Liza, on the other hand, seems to have turned into a statue, and only stops staring at Marcus when Isabel demands her attention.

Marcus definitely has a fan there; but he's still looking shocked and I don't feel it's fair to point out that one of Nessa's family is currently starstruck.

Maybe she can get an autograph later.

And I'm sure Isa will show her how to do the perfect selfie with Marcus if she feels the need later on . . .

Instead, I tell Marcus: 'I've got a blanket in the Visitors' Hut. If you can't beat them, join them is what I say. I can't promise food, but we can have a coffee.'

'Sounds great,' he says, and I feel his fingers brush mine. I move mine a little so they are entwined in his and we squeeze each other's hands before letting them drop.

Fae has located a picnic blanket from the depths of her basket and begins unfolding it. She indicates that Alfie should take the other corners, so they can spread it out properly. He does as he's bid, then moves back a bit to get a better space under the old chestnut tree. Suddenly, Alfie stands stock-still, frozen in place, gripping the picnic blanket until his knuckles show white through his skin. Then the colour drains from his face and he seems to cease functioning.

'Oh God,' he says. 'Oh dear God. No. Please, no!'

Then all our mobile phones ping at once. Every single one of them, including mine. Everyone peers at where their phones are, and there's a sort of mass movement as everyone pulls them out of bags and pockets.

I gently leave go of Maggie's sticky little hand, and do the same; and I can feel my eyes widen as I look at what's just come through.

It's a photo.

Of Schubert.

And on one paw he's sporting a pink bootie, and on the other he's sporting a blue bootie. On his head is a floppy, white baby bonnet.

There's also a bib around his neck, and it proclaims: "Big Brother!"

'Oh my God!' I hold the phone out to Marcus and his eyes widen. Then the place erupts into cheers (from the women) and groans of anguish (from the menfolk).

'I knew it, I just knew it. Fae! Fae! Why did I have to see that? I can never unsee it! I saw it before she told us! Why me? Why?' howls Alfie. 'And that picture. Bloody Schubert! In a bloody bonnet. He'll need even more babysitting now! This is hellish. It's hellish!'

'It's your twinny thing.' Fae pats his knee. 'You know you always see these things. The time to worry,' she says with a wicked twinkle in her eye, 'is when I pull the same stunt. But I can't think of a way to top this one.'

Alfie looks even more horrified, and I bite my lip and hide a smile as she bursts out laughing and hugs him. 'No,' she says. 'Don't worry. Not for a while yet!'

Nessa and Ewan have been swallowed up by a swarm of well-wishers, and I hurry over to hug her and offer my congratulations. 'Is it twins?' I can't help asking. 'With the two different booties and stuff?'

Nessa laughs and shakes her head. 'Not this time,' she says. 'I just don't know what it'll be. So Schubert advised me to cover my bases.'

'Not this time?' Ewan is quick to pick up on that one and turns to her. 'What — so next time it might be?' He looks terrified, poor bloke, as well he might. 'Like — twins?'

'Hmmm. Let's get this one out of the way first,' says Nessa and throws her arms around him, laughing.

'She didn't answer,' whispers Marcus in my ear. 'She evaded the question.'

'Yes — sometimes that can happen. You don't always get the full picture at first. People can be quite good at evading things.' I turn to him and grin, so he knows I'm teasing. I hold my hand out. 'Come on. I want to go back to the Temple. I think we were in the middle of something?'

So we slip away, and hurry back along the winding paths the way we came as the excited chatter fades away behind us.

The Temple is blissfully cool and quiet inside — but there is almost the sense of someone having just left. I hear footsteps outside and a tuneless humming, and I look at Marcus. He looks a little worried, but I just smile and stick my head out of the door.

Maggie is wandering around collecting wildflowers and she catches sight of me and blows me a kiss.

'I'm getting these for Aunty Nessa, and for my new baby cousin,' she tells me, holding the posy aloft. 'Bertie told me my baby cousin was coming. I knewed it before everyone else. I'm very happy to be getting a new baby cousin.'

'Then Bertie knows who he can trust,' I tell her.

Maggie nods seriously. Her eyes drift towards one of the other doors of the Temple; the one that faces up towards the house. She smiles as her gaze follows something I can't see. 'Lady Clemmie is happy too,' she says. 'She likes this place a lot.'

I do admit to a little shiver at this point. 'Well, I'm ever so delighted about that.'

Then there's a rustle and a thunk and Schubert appears out of the undergrowth. 'Mow wow?' he says, and Maggie nods again.

'I come now,' she says. She blows me another kiss, and the pair of them run off, Maggie holding her posy in the air like a spear and yelling war cries as she jogs after Schubert.

I gently close the door and lean my back against it. 'I think we're alone,' I say.

'Are you sure?' Marcus comes over to me and takes my hand, drawing me back to the centre of the room.

'I'm sure. I think Clemmie's gone too. Back to Glentavish House.'

This time Marcus does shiver. 'Then I'm pleased I'm here instead. Anyway — I'm thinking of doing some work in the gardens at Glentavish. So I might need a Head Gardener at some point.'

'Oh?' I look at him curiously. 'Is that the only reason you decided to make up with me? So I could sort your weedy old garden out?'

159

'Not at all!' He looks at me all innocently, and I can't help but laugh, because I know he's teasing. But wow — if I could get my hands on that estate . . . bring it back to what it was when Clemmie was around. I could do so, so much in there. But there's my Garden to look after as well — so it may be just a daydream.

'It does sound perfect. But the commute.' I pull a face. 'I mean, I know the ideal person, but they've got a business to run and a flat which is too far away to be practical. For travelling purposes.'

'I think I could perhaps make a Gardener's Cottage out of the stables. My project manager will no longer be on-site — the whole project could well be finished by then, so I'll have some space.' There's a twinkle in his eye and I know he's teasing again as he speaks the next words. 'The resident might have to put up with the odd yogi wandering around or retreating, though — perhaps. In the future. But it's just a thought. In reality, if ever I got a gardener, they might like to be on-site a lot of the time. Not just to work, obviously, but to be, I don't know, closer to their own job as well. I hear the landlord is away a lot of the time, so it would be nice and peaceful for them. Nobody to bother them too much. It makes the proposition more attractive, doesn't it? If there's board and lodging available.'

'And I'm sure the landlord will come up as much as he can,' I say. 'In between jobs. Rather than lurking around, I don't know, Islington, perhaps? I mean, he has a big job to finish here anyway. The Temple won't build itself. But the gardener will be fine with whatever the landlord can manage. And perhaps, in the future, the odd yogi. It's a risk she'd be willing to take.'

'You make a good point,' he says, and we lock eyes with one another.

I know this isn't going to be easy. I know, if our ideas pan out, that I'll miss him like crazy, and that he'll miss me too. I just knewed it, as Maggie would say.

But it might work — it might work, if we both give it a fair chance.

The prospect is, as they say, appealing.

We continue to look at one another for a moment, and I feel my lips twitching into a smile. 'You know how I said I might forgive you someday?' I find myself saying. 'I think, actually, someday has come.'

'Was it bribery and corruption that made you come to that decision?' he asks.

I shake my head. 'No. It's the fact that I think we have a chance. I really do. And I think it's what Glentavish wants as well.'

'And your Garden?'

'And my Garden. For definite.'

Then we finally, finally, lean into one another and kiss. And it's just as good as I imagined it would be.

And this time, nothing will come between us.

And eventually, as I open my eyes and come back to my senses, I catch a glimpse through the window of a dark-haired woman running up the lawn towards Glentavish House. Her feet are bare, and she's holding up the hem of her dress; then she stops and throws her arms in the air and dances on the lawn until she fades from sight.

'Clemmie?' he asks me.

'Clemmie,' I say. 'And I think she's just given us her blessing.'

Then we kiss again as the roses burst into bloom, one by one, outside the windows of our little piece of heaven on earth.

THE END

THANK YOU

Thank you so much for reading, and hopefully enjoying, Bea's Magical Summer Garden. I also hope you agree that it is indeed a magical place and that Schubert, as always, has put his paw print firmly on the story, and that Bea and Marcus are worthy beneficiaries of his mystical meddling.

However, authors need to know they are doing the right thing, and keeping our readers happy is a huge part of the job. So, it would be wonderful if you could find a moment just to write a quick review on the website where you bought the book, just to let me know that you enjoyed it. Thank you once again, and do feel free to contact me at any time on Facebook, Twitter, through my website (details on following page), or through my lovely publishers, Choc Lit.

Much love to you all,

Kirsty

xx

THE CHOC LIT STORY

Established in 2009, Choc Lit is an independent, award-winning publisher dedicated to creating a delicious selection of quality women's fiction.

We have won 18 awards, including Publisher of the Year and the Romantic Novel of the Year, and have been shortlisted for countless others.

All our novels are selected by genuine readers. We are proud to publish talented first-time authors, as well as established writers whose books we love introducing to a new generation of readers.

In 2023, we became a Joffe Books company. Best known for publishing a wide range of commercial fiction, Joffe Books has its roots in women's fiction. Today it is one of the largest independent publishers in the UK.

We love to hear from you, so please email us about absolutely anything bookish at

choc-lit@joffebooks.com

If you want to receive free books every Friday and hear about all our new releases, join our mailing list here.

www.choc-lit.com